down the bath rocks

a boy's own penny wonder

Patrick
O'Connor

GILL AND MACMILLAN

Published by
GILL AND MACMILLAN LTD
2 Belvedere Place
Dublin 1

and in London through association with the
MACMILLAN
group of publishing companies

7171 0530 X

Jacket designed by Hilliard Hayden

Printed and bound in the Republic of Ireland by
CAHILL & CO LIMITED DUBLIN 8

Seeking a family name for the Irish immigrants of this novel, it occurred to me that I need look no further than under my nose, as it were, and that I may as well use my pre-eminently generic first name also—the better, into the bargain, to identify with and get under the skin of the character who tells the story.

Nevertheless, I must emphasise that the PATRICK O'CONNOR of the tale is merely a literary invention as fictitious as all the other characters in the book who bear no relation whatsoever to real people, living or dead.

But there is always the chance that this work of fiction, set in the twenties, may throw some light on the factual back-street life of that time.

PATRICK O'CONNOR, London, 1971.

For my Mother where she is

PART I

I

My sister Mary's hair was red but her face was white with ferntickles all over it. She knelt down on the carpet in front of the fire, bowed her head and let her long hair trail on the floor. Toby the cat got up on his hind legs and pawed at it.

She took me down the Bath Rocks on my go-chair with Lizzie Boyle and Margit Morgan and Annie. We went along, bumping over the big stones in the Inches Road, past the billboards and round by Mick Kelly the bookie's hut. Trains puffed past on their way to the harbour. The Arran Boat Train was an express and we all waved to the faces going past. They were going on their holidays to Arran. But not the Belfast Boat Train because that didn't come past till night-time.

I looked down at the bubbles in the tar and sometimes a wheel of the go-chair would drive right through one and burst it. I could see little beasties down among the stones and flies would get caught in the tar.

I could hear the horns of the boats blowing in the harbour and the riveting in the shipyard going all the time.

Mary stopped my go-chair near the muck dump where I saw down to the rocks and smelt burning. Margit Morgan and Lizzie Boyle and Mary and my sister Annie too were laughing and Annie picked me up and lifted me high up into the air where the big white birds were with claws and sharp beaks. I began to cry and they took me home again to my mammy. The gates were shut because a train was going through and when they opened we had to run across because if we didn't a train would come and run us over. The jiggling up and down of the go-chair wheels on the railway lines hurt my face and I was crying even more

When we got home, my mammy took me into a corner and made a noise like a pigeon and opened up her white blouse and took out her diddy and put the end in my mouth. I stopped crying because it was like sucking a sweetie. When I looked up her eyes were shining down at me over the gold locket swinging in the sun.

One day m'mammy held me between her legs while she sat on the chair beside the fire and we listened and then we heard my daddy's heavy boots coming up the wooden stairs to the attic. When we got to the door and began to open it, she said

–Now Patrick, now go on, walk to your daddy!

And I staggered across the floor to him and he caught me just as I got between his big moleskinned legs and swung me high into the air, right up to the ceiling. I looked at the cracks and pictures and spiders when I was up there. Then just as the spider was coming out I went down again with the air blowing up my pinnie.

I cried and girned for short trousers as soon as I could walk because wearing pinnies is like a lassie. And when I got my trousers and stockings with stripes at the tops and lacing boots instead of button boots and a woollen jersey, I could pull a chair over to the window and climb up on it and look out.

I was nearly dizzy when I looked out of the attic window over the slates and beside me the chimley was smoking, the same one that they said I came down when I was born. You could see the Inches Road where I used to go in my go-chair and the rubbish dump and the Flute Band hut and the sea and the bathing pond across the bay and a bit of the Bath Rocks and a big shunting yard with trains in it and Christie's Yard with Harry England's cottage and the back doors of the Fenian Row and Missus Cosgrove's yard where she kept the hens and Paddy's Milestone on the sea and a boat smoking away out where there were no waves.

The Glen Sannox was coming over from Troon, getting

nearer and nearer until you could see the white waves at the bow but when it was getting right up it disappeared behind the chimleys of the Fenian Row. You couldn't see Mick Kelly's hut because that was hidden behind the Church of the Nazarene.

There was only me and my mammy left in the house after Mary and Annie had gone to school. John was out looking for work and my daddy was out working. Bridget wasn't there because she was living with my auntie in Londonderry. My mammy got a piece of old cloth, put the end in the fire to light it, then tramped on it to put it out. She gave it to me when the smoke was coming from it and asked me to swing it backwards and forwards. When there was a lot of smoke in the attic and more coming, she got out the po and took it behind the bed. When I stood swinging the cloth backwards and forwards with the smoke coming from it just like the altar boys in the chapel, she sat on the po behind the end of the big bed where I couldn't see her. When she was finished sitting on the po, she opened the door to see if there was anybody coming and when no-one was there, she put the po under her apron and carried it down the wooden stairs, then down the stone steps with the iron rail, then down to the closet at the end of the backyard where she emptied it. When she came back she took the cloth from me and put it in the fire and told me it was a wee secret. I'm not to tell anybody, not even my daddy. Then she began polishing the brass knobs on the big bed so hard she was red in the face. It took a long time for the smell of the smoke to go away.

I asked her if I could go out to play and she said I wasn't to go too far away because it would soon be dinner time. I went down the wooden stairs from the attic, jumping over the lumps of brown and yellow number two done by the McGraw children from the attic across the landing from ours. M'mammy told my daddy they were dirty buggers, they were always doing number two on the stairs. Then I went through the next landing between the Boyles and the Brannifs. I stopped to look through a hole cut in the wooden side. You could see into the Morgans' backyard over the wall. One of Missus Cosgrove's hens had wandered away from its nest and was scratching around the rubbish bucket. I came on to the stone steps and stopped on the first bit before the steps turn round. I could put my head through the railings and look down into the backyard. I looked down on the bricks to see if there were any worms coming up through the cracks. I couldn't see any and I didn't get my head stuck in the railings. Robert Cook shouted to me from McNamee's backyard next door. He wanted me to come and play at bools. I said

–Aye, I'm coming round!

I went down the last stone steps, through the close and out into the street. Old Sailor McFarlane was sitting on his window sill in the sun. His wooden leg was sticking out a bit on to the pavement and his walking sticks were beside him.

I stopped to look at him as he was snedding tobacco to put in his pipe with his knife which was a great one with a long bent handle made of bone. His big brass buckle was glinting in the sun and above that I could see his sailor's jersey, blue woollen with flags across it and words. He wore a peaked sailor's bunnet and he had a big white twirly moustache and his eyes were blue too and crinkly around the edges. He always laughed at me and shook his head and I liked being near him to smell the tobacco smell and a kind of tangle which hung around him. He lost his leg in the sea.

I waited till he had finished snedding his tobacco and putting it in his pipe and lighting it with a match and puffing away. Then he patted me on the head and gave me a halfpenny because it was Friday and I went away on down the street past the Harveys and the Boyces and turned into the Big Pen.

Robert Cook had already made the square for bools; it was easy for him for they had a yard of black dirt and ours is made of bricks. I had my bag of bools in my pocket and I told him I got a halfpenny from Sailor McFarlane. He said

–Spend it. Go on, spend it, what are you going to buy?

–Will I get a halfpenny's worth of broken toffee from Brekenridge's? She gives you a lot. Or caramels, you get four a halfpenny in McAteer's wee shop and they last long. He said

–A sooker! And give me a sook, from P. Marron's or soor plooms or Ogie-Pogie Eyes that change colours as you suck them and you can take them out and look at them.

–A candy apple!

–You won't be able to give me some . . .

–I'll give you a bite.

We started to laugh and once we started we couldn't stop. He said he'd give me a bite then he ran after me as if he was a lion. I turned round and said I'd give him a bite and ran after him like a monster.

–*Hi, Jock McCuddy!*
Mah cuddy's o'er the dyke
If you touch mah cuddy,
Mah cuddy will gi'e you a bite!

We ran around the yard singing this and shouting I'll gi'e you a bite then Robert Cook fell over the brick path that leads from the big pen to the closets, you have to have a key to open them. He skinned his knee a bit but he didn't cry. Then we went to McAteer's shop to buy a sherbet sooker and I opened up the paper and gave him some sherbet to lick and a bit of the allycreesh. There was a prize inside, a diamond ring and I put this in my hip pocket to give to Mary for her treasure.

We were sitting on Missus Cook's back window sill, sometimes she chases you away but sometimes she is not in, she's out for the messages. I gave him four bools for a glassie and he gave me four for a plunker. He had a great leadie and I said I would give him two glassies and a plunker for it but he wouldn't take them, he said it was a beater. You could skin everybody with it.

While we were sitting there we began to smell cabbage from the pot and tatties being boiled. Missus Cook came in with the messages and chased us away from the window sill. We ran round the yard again singing and putting our arms out like wings.

–Wee chookie birdie tol-ol-ol,
Left an egg on the window soal!

Then I heard the screek of ropes in a window being lifted high up and I knew it was m'mammy before I heard her calling

–Patrick, come up and get your dinner!

Then Granny McNamee came out for Robert and stood in the Big Pen and put her hands on her big hips and called

–Raberd Jahn Cook!
Raberd Jahn Cook!

so that you could hear her all over the street. Other people opened their windows and shouted

–Away you and Raberd Jahn Cook!

and a lot of wee boys shouted

–Raberd Jahn Cook, Raberd Jahn Cook!

and Robert hung down his head and wouldn't go in and Granny McNamee had to chase him. That gave me the chance to slip past her so that she wouldn't give me a clink on the ear and I ran through the Big Pen, listening to my boots ringing and I went in for my dinner.

2

After dinner, m'mammy said to come on we would go for a wee run into Saltcoats and she put on her shawl and locked the attic door with the key. She carried me in the shawl down Bute Place and into Princes Street and we went over to beside Mary Barbour's Toy Shop where the cabs were standing. We climbed up steps at the back and through a wee door and the driver cracked his whip, the horse turned right round, we went down Princes Street through the Railway Gates, past the English Church and along the road beside the shore to Saltcoats. The cabs were made of brown wood and you sat round the side and you could lean out over and watch the road going past and the wheels going round. I managed to get up on the seat and look right over so that I could see the horse although mammy was holding me down. The horse's hooves were trotting then they slowed down to a walk then suddenly it stopped and its tail shot up straight in front of the driver's seat and after a while when its tail went down again everybody began to laugh and the driver said something sideways, spat brown juice on to the road and cracked his whip.

We passed a great big cross on the green in front of the promenade. My mammy said

–Look, Patrick, there's the Cannon Hill!

and pointed up a hill with a castle on top of it. A train was puffing along at the bottom of the hill. I wanted to look the other way where the sun was shining on the sea and silver fish were doing the shimmy.

The cabs all stopped at the La Scala picture house and stood in line. We got down and the driver stood at the back helping us out and collecting money. He had a big red nose and a moustache like my daddy's but not as big.

M'mammy let me walk and held me by the hand and we went round the shops. I wanted to look at all the toys but she kept pulling me away. I just looked at the legs and feet as we went along, the big lacing boots of the men and the strap button shoes of the women. Some of the women wore button boots with buttons all up the side. We have a button-hook in the house for hooking them on. Sometimes a button comes off and you have to go to the cobbler to get it put on with a machine.

There were caramel papers lying about among the saw-dust on the floor of Lipton's. There were bits of broken biscuits and a bit of ham and a smashed egg and a big wet part in the sawdust. There was a lump of caramel in one of the papers and I bent down to pick it up and eat it and my mammy said that was dirty, dirty, ah, ah, and knocked it out of my hand. She said to look, look, look what the man was doing and I looked up at a man with a white apron and black buttons who was cutting ham with a long knife and I watched the sharp blade of the knife slicing through the ham. I told my mammy I wanted a knife like that.

I shouted

–Mammy, I want to pee! Mammy, I want to pee!

–Sh! Sh!

Her face got red and she took me by the hand and ran out of the shop, past the Buttercup Dairy, down a passage-way to a big empty space where the merry-go-rounds and the hobby horses that go up and down come to. Then she held me and I did a pee on the stones.

In Countess Street there was a well where I had a drink from an iron cup with a chain on it. The water tasted like when you put a leadie in your mouth. Mammy let me watch the horses having a drink from the trough. The coal cart horse. The milkman's horse. The baker's horse. The old donkey of the man who collects rags, bones and jam jars. He comes down our street and shouts

–Any old stocking rags! Any old woollen rags!
A suitable toy for a girl or a boy!

If you take him out some jam jars or old stockings he gives

you a flying canary on the end of a string with a stick to hold it that whistles as you whirl it round your head. If you have a great lot of old rags you can get a goldfish.

Coming back in the brown cab the wind was blowing in from the shore and my mammy put her shawl over her head and tucked me inside it and the driver had his coat collar turned up and the horse was snortering and he cracked his whip and made it trot fast.

When we got home we put all the messages on the table. The sugar bag burst and we had to lift it all up with a spoon. Then mammy said she'd make a wee cup of tea and we had a rhubarb tart each that she bought in Saltcoats. Then I played with bools in front of the fender. A cry came up from the street.

–Parryfin!
Parreefin!

then he rang his big bell.

–Par-ee-fin!
Par-ee-fin!

M'mammy took the can and said to me I was not to go near the fire and ran down the stairs and came back with a can of paraffin for the lamp.

Mary and Annie came in from school and sat down and played with me. They were showing me pictures in the fire when m'mammy said

–That's your daddy's foot on the stairs.

She sent Annie out to Coyles to get the fish suppers then we heard his big boots clumping up the stairs. I went to the door to meet him and catch his hand and Toby the cat stuck its tail up and ran over to the door as if it had seen a mouse.

Then he came round the door and bent down and caught hold of me and swung me up to the ceiling where I saw the same spider. Then he held me in front of his big black eyes and I could smell a kind of tangle from his moustache. When he put me down he put his hands in his moleskin trouser pocket and said to me

–Is this what you want? Is this what you're looking for? and gave me a big brown penny. He gave Mary one too and we went away in to a corner and showed each other the numbers on them and Mary told me what they were.

Later that night before I went to sleep I heard mammy saying to my daddy that she had taken me on the horse cab in the afternoon. She said she wanted me to go on one, they wouldn't be there long because of the new motor buses. She said I might not get a chance to see a brown horse cab again and m'daddy said

–Aye, but I suppose he'll see plenty of the black ones!

3

I heard my mammy saying I was a good wee boy so I said to John

–John, wash the good wee boy's face . . . John . . . Wash the good wee boy's face.

Annie was giggling but mammy was saying sh, and daddy was saying sh, hen. But John was laughing too as he washed my face from a basin of water in front of the attic window. He got the water from the white pail where you get a drink, not the black pail for the slops and the tea leaves and sometimes you pee in. John said

–I've always got to go down for a pail of water, I'm always going down for a pail of water, can nobody else go down and get a pail of water except me?

And m'daddy said, sh, son, and I said

–John, wash the good wee boy's face!

He started to laugh again and he let the soap go in my eyes. When my face was washed and I had my woollen jersey on and a striped tie and striped stockings and my boots polished, my mammy said

–You can go down to Boyles' landing and play, son.

I went down the stairs and there was a lot of people coming up and down. Some of them were saying tut, tut, tut, because the McGraws had dirtied the stair again and they tramped on it and they were lifting up their boots and shoes to look at the soles and saying tut, tut, tut.

Doctor McCann came with his bag and m'mammy came down halfway to meet him and said to watch his feet on the stairs. He patted my head as he went past and bent down and looked at my face and said

–That's wee Patrick, isn't it?

I asked Annie if Mary was coming down to play and she said Mary was in the bed that Missus Brannif lent us.

I went up the stairs again to look for Mary and she wasn't in the big bed where she sleeps with me and my mammy and Annie and sometimes Bridget when she is here. She wasn't in the set-in bed where my daddy and John sleep. She was in this bed that Missus Brannif lent to us. There were white curtains along the rail at the bottom and there was a big crowd of people round it. I could smell wintergreen and I could see the white po under the bed through their legs. Doctor McCann was talking to m'mammy and then he went through the crowd of people to the bed with tubes coming out of his ears. I asked m'mammy if I could go in the bed with Mary and she said

–No, my wee son, go you down the stairs and play with Annie.

Her eyes were a bit watery.

4

It was getting dark and I said to John

–John, lift me up to see the choogh trains.

He said it was getting too dark but he would lift me up to see the lights. He lifted me up to look out the window and some houses were lighting up in the Fenian Row. The gas lamp came on in Morgans' backyard. I could see a lamp on the Inches Road and a big light at Battery Point. Over behind the Bath Rocks I could see lights all along the South Beach and the lights of the Bathing Pond. John pointed away far away and said

–Look, there's the lights of Troon, they are winking.

And those away even farther he said were the lights of Ayr and this light was flashing out and in and a ray was going through the sky and he said that was the lighthouse on Paddy's Milestone.

I jiggled to get down again and I turned round to look at all the people kneeling down in the room. There were candles lit on the mantelpiece and candles lit on the table where there was a big long white box. It was made of white shiny cloth like the shoes I saw Mary wearing once. I asked John where Mary was and he said she was away for a visit. I said where was that, and he said

–Here, do you want a glassie? I've got a glassie for you!

The women all had their faces washed and the big men's boots were all polished and they all had beads hanging from their fingers. They were all kneeling around the room and some were kneeling by the open door and some were kneeling by the big bed and some were nearly under the set-in bed and some were nearly in the fire and some were down the stairs outside the door. My mammy bent her head down and looked at the beads in her hand and said something out loud.

When she stopped all the people kneeling down began to murmur and hum. When they stopped my mammy said something again then they all murmured after her.

I tried to get to m'mammy and daddy kneeling together and I fell over a big man's legs then I fell over a big woman's legs then m'mammy caught me. I said

–Where's Mary?

–Sh, son, she's gone away. Sh.

Some women began to cry.

They all got up from their knees and I was in among all the legs again like in the Plantation Woods. M'daddy had a bottle and he was giving the men a drink from it in cups and tumblers. I smelt the same tangle that comes from his moustache. Some of the big men smoked pipes and they would go over and spit in the fire. Old Micky Boyle from downstairs was there and he had a collar and tie on. Women were talking away in the corners. Mammy was making tea and giving them buttered scones. I got a jam scone and a drink of lemonade.

Mister McCanse who goes around with the fresh herrings in the mornings began to sing. Micky Boyle spat in the fire and said to give us *Kathleen Mavourneen.*

My eyes began to nip with the tobacco smoke and I went over to smell the empty bottles in the corner. Three men were singing different songs all at the same time. Some women were still crying. Two girls were dancing in a corner.

You couldn't hear the McGraws fighting next door.

Mister McCanse fell down the stairs. I fell asleep in John's lap.

The hens were chooking in Missus Cosgrove's backyard and I said

–John, lift the good wee boy up to see the chooky hens.

–Only for a wee while because I've got to go out and get the rolls for the breakfast.

But I went sailing up past the top window pane and I saw some white hens in the yard before I came down again and then he went for the rolls.

Annie came and washed my face and m'daddy was lighting the fire then I played with the cat for a while with a bit of string and a bit of paper tied to the end. John came in with the rolls and we had our breakfast then m'mammy cleared all the things away quickly. Daddy shaved himself near the window in front of a looking glass and m'mammy had on her best costume. There was a funny smell of wintergreen and flowers and like the taste of the leadie in my mouth.

Big men began to come up and down the stairs and this time some of them had black hats on. M'mammy said I could go and play on the stairs so I went down to Boyles' landing and looked through the hole to see if I could spy any chooky hens. Big men in blue suits were passing by and patting me on the head and one stopped and opened up his jacket where there was a big gold chain across his waistcoat. He took out his watch and the rim jumped open and I could hear it ticking. Then he put his hand in his pocket and gave me two pennies, telling me to give one to my sister. Another man passed by and he gave me a halfpenny. Then another gave me a penny. Another gave me twopence and one gave me a silver threepenny bit and I was putting it all in my pocket.

Then I slipped down the stone steps and out the close and as I went through I could hear horses snortering and a hoof ringing on the street. When I went out there was a black cab with glass windows all round like a shop and in the shafts a great big black horse. A beater. A beauty.

It was playing with its hoof a bit and there was a black feather sticking up from its head like one of the Indians in the pictures. There were other black cabs lined up with other black horses but not beaters like this one. This one was mine.

All the people in the street were looking out of their windows and some were standing in the doors with their arms folded and shawls around them and everybody was saying sh, to their weans. I turned to go back through the close but met four big men with hats carrying the long white box on their shoulders walking slowly along, their feet staggering a bit as they came round the corner from the stone steps. I had to squeeze against the wall as they went past. My mammy and daddy came after them and big men and women in their good clothes and they all squeezed me against the wall as they went past as if they couldn't see me and I had to jump up on Missus Taylor's step.

I shoved my way out of the close to the street and I saw the four men putting the white box in the black cab with windows like a shop. Then they closed a glass door at the back and you could see the white box sitting inside among the flowers. It looked as if it was iced like the christening cakes that you see in the baker's window.

There was a crowd of people all around now and two of the men with hats climbed up and one took the reins of the big black horse. M'mammy and daddy went into another black cab and I broke through the crowd shouting

–Mammy! Daddy!

I wanted to go with them in the cab. But John came and caught me and lifted me up to see them and my daddy gave me another penny and my mammy said

–Sh, Patrick, my wee son.

We went back to the close and all the cabs began to move away slowly and Sailor McFarlane took his cap off and looked closely at the ground and Sarah Brannif was crying and when all the horses and cabs had turned the corner there was a lot of dung left in the street.

5

My mammy said it was time to go to bed now and I said to her

–Where's Mary gone . . . where's the nice white box?

–Mary's on her way to heaven in the white box.

–Where's heaven?

–Up there in the sky.

I asked John to take me over to the window to see the sky and I looked up and you could see all the stars, some of them winking.

–Is that where heaven is?

–Yes.

–Is that where Mary's going?

–Yes.

I looked among the stars in all directions to see the white box going through to heaven but it must have been well on its way because I couldn't find it anywhere.

But I had a lot of pennies and halfpennies and one silver threepenny bit. It was a great morning. A beezer. Before I went to sleep I made a wish that a lot more would want to go to heaven in their box soon, so that I could get some more.

6

I was down in the backyard playing in the water around the spicket with Robert Cook and Robert and Alec Taylor. The water wasn't running away because the hole was stopped up with dirt and tea leaves and vegetables. It made a great pond to sail your boats in. Mine was the Glen Sannox. Robert and Alec Taylor wanted the Atalanta and they were fighting, then their sister Letty came out and pulled them apart and told Alec that he could be the Juno for that was a paddle steamer so he was the Juno. Robert Cook said

–What will I be? I wanted to be the Juno.

Letty said

–You can go back and play in your own backyard, Raberd Jahn Cook, Raberd Jahn Cook!

I said

–You be the King Orry, Robert. . . You be the Isle of Man Boat.

–No, I'll be the Belfast Boat because my uncle works at it.

So he was the Belfast Boat and Robert Taylor was the Atalanta and Alec was the Juno and I was the Glen Sannox.

We howked two bricks out of the backyard with an old spoon that the McGraws had left lying about then we made stepping stones through the water and we got up to the brass spicket on them and turned it on and made the water come scooshing out. This made a storm for the boats. Then it became a great pond, it got bigger and bigger and there were waves like down the shore and the storm got worse and the Belfast boat sank.

Missus Brannif shouted down from her window

–Turn that water aff!

and I tried and Alec tried but we couldn't turn it off and my jersey was soaken and we heard the shipyard horn going for the men's dinner and after a while Robert and Alec's daddy, Sanny Taylor, came home for his dinner. Sanny Taylor is a riveter and he plays inside right for the Winton Rovers and he scored two goals on Saturday against Kilbirnie Ladeside and he came out and turned the water off.

I was going up for my dinner and Alec Taylor and Robert Cook asked me was I coming down the shore after to catch crabs and I said I would ask. I went up the stairs and my mammy said

–Look at you, you're soaken wet!

She took my jersey off and my boots and stockings and trousers and I had my dinner, fried slice and a dipped piece of bread.

After my dinner I said

–Can I go down the shore with Alec Taylor to catch crabs?

–No, your clothes are soaken!

They were hanging in front of the fire with steam coming out of them like the kettle when it is boiling.

I began to girn because she would not let me go down the shore.

–Stop your girning! Go and play with the cat. Look, he's pining away because he misses Mary.

Toby the cat was up on the big bed at the bit where Mary used to lie and his eyes looked at me as if he was crying. I tried to play with him but he wouldn't play, not even with a bit of string with a paper tied to it and when I climbed up on the bed, he jumped down and went over and lay in front of the fire on the bit where Mary used to let him play with her hair. Sometimes he got up and stood with his tail up and looked at the bed and my mammy said

–I think cats see things, you know. The poor wee thing is pining away, so he is.

That's what Mary used to say to me. She used to pat me on the head and cuddle me and say

–Ah poor wee thing. What's the matter, Patty?

M'mammy let me look out of the window and said not to lean too far out and Robert Cook and Alec and Robert

Taylor and Eddie McAteer were down in the Big Pen and they shouted up

–Are you coming down the shore to catch crabs?

They had glass jam jars for catching them in.

–No, m'mammy won't let me come out because I got m'clothes wet!

They began to charge round the pen shouting

–His mammy won't let him come out because he got his clothes wet! Hullaw! Hullaw! He can't come out! He can't come out!

Then they went away. I shouted I would come out after and they shouted back all right.

So I just looked out the window, down the backyard. Do'e-Do'e Donaldson came through with another two pigeons that he had caught and took a short cut over our wall into the Fenian Row and put the pigeons in his Do'e Hut. If you go over to our grate when the fire is out and listen up the chimley you can hear the pigeons going oocklacoo, oocklacoo.

The tide was going out, down the Inches, and you could see the Wee Cruiben Rock and then the Big Cruiben Rock was coming out of the sea, more and more. I kidded on I was a boat and scooshed through the sea away out from the Big Cruiben to Paddy's Milestone then I saw the Atlanta away far away coming from Ayr. I looked up at the smoke coming out of the chimley, it was going right up to the sky and when I saw the sky it made me feel a bit dizzy and I looked at the slates on the roof and thought I was rolling down and hanging on to the gutter then falling off the roof and smashing to pieces. So I turned and put my head in the attic again and my mammy had her clothes up and was putting on a pair of long knickers the same colour as the sky.

–Look out the window, look at the chooky hens!

I turned and looked out again and I saw Robert Cook and Alec and Robert Taylor going round by the Flute Band Hut, carrying their jam jars. And they had Letty Taylor with them. She always laughs at me and gives me a sweetie or a suck from her sooker and she always has nice clean pinnies with flowers in them and a coloured ribbon in her hair.

When I saw Letty I began to winge again and my mammy said to come here son and she lifted me up in her arms and sat with me on her knees in front of the fire and rocked me backwards and forwards and I could hear the pigeons up the chimley going oocklacoo, oocklacoo and I went to sleep.

When I woke up, John was in.

–Tell me a story, John, g'on, tell me a story.

He said to wait a wee while. He had to go out to Stark's to get tobacco for m'daddy's pipe and the *Weekly News* and the *Red Letter* and the *Wizard* and we pay on Friday.

When he came back he showed me the comic cuts. Spadger's Eleven and Casey's Court and the Cheery Chinks and Nosey Parker and Slippery Sam.

Then I climbed up on his knee and he told me the story about his ranch in the Rocky Mountains where he has a horse and cowboys. He's got one for me too. It's called Silver King and it is a white pony. I'm to have a belt with silver studs and cart wheels on it and a gun. My gun has got a pearl handle and he will teach me how to draw it fast from my holster so that I can shoot the bad yins. I can have a star as well and I'm to be the sheriff. He is to be the deputy and Robert Cook and Robert and Alec Taylor and Eddie and James McAteer and a lot more will be the posse. And I will rescue Letty Taylor but I didn't tell John this.

–You better hurry up and grow up big so that I can take you to the ranch!

My mammy washed me in front of the fire before putting me to bed and I was looking at the calendar hanging beside the mantelpiece. She said

–It's nineteen twenty-five, did you know that? It's nineteen twenty-five. And do you know what that means? You're five years of age and next week you'll be going to school.

–I don't want to go to school.

–Oh, but everybody has to go to school.

I nearly began to girn but I managed to stop it when it got to my throat.

I could hear the wind whistling around the attic and making noises in the chimley and the rain spattering and running down the window. Daddy and mammy were saying that there was a storm tonight, aye, there was a storm tonight. I wanted to coory up in my bed. When I was ready my daddy bent down in front of me and John lifted me up on the chair and I climbed on my daddy's back and he put his arms under my legs and I put my arms around his neck. Then he began to go up and down like a horse and he said

–Get up oul horsy, go for gran!

–Get up oul horsy, go for gran!

He went all round the table and over to the coalhouse in the corner by the door and then turned and he was saying

–Get up oul horsy, go for gran!

Then he was over by the bed and he turned and lowered me down and said

–Oho, a bag of coals, here's your bag of coals, missus!

and I laughed and I didn't want to girn anymore.

M'mammy came and tucked me into the bed and said

–Now stay in your wee corner Patrick and make room for your sister and me.

And I cooried down under the clothes and listened to the wind making a noise like a ghost in the chimley and the door rattling and the waves pounding over the big wall on the Inches Road. The lamp had gone down lower and I heard the boats blowing their horns in the distance. I wanted to go away on the boats and not go to school. The horn of a big boat blew as if it was just over the roofs of the Fenian Row and it sounded sad and my daddy said that was Wullie Brannif away to sea again and my mammy said

–Aye, God help him poor soul on a night like this.

7

The comb hurt my head as it was pulled through my hair.

–Don't winge son, I'll soon be finished but we've got to race or you'll miss the motor, Annie is ready and Lizzie Boyle is calling up the stairs.

I had a new jersey on with a striped tie and a pair of new boots and a school-bag with straps with buttered rolls in it for my dinner and playtime.

–More haste less speed. Look, your trousers are not buttoned up the front!

Annie said

–Hurry up, we'll miss the motor, mammy!

Then we ran down the stairs and out the close and Annie and Lizzie took my hands on each side and ran with me. Most of the time my feet were off the ground and I was flying through the air like a bird or as if I was on a swing as we turned the corner into Bute Place past the Church of the Nazarene then round the corner at the Union Bank of Scotland and across Princes Street. There was a big crowd outside the Princes Picture House waiting for Mick Kelly's school bus and they were all yelling and chasing and hitting each other. Annie said

–Come on you over Patrick and stand in this corner and you won't get knocked down.

–I want to see the pictures in the glass case, what are they?

–It's Tom Mix and Tony his horse in the continued picture.

–What's the big picture?

–Metro Polis.

–What kind of Polis are they? Not the same as the Ardrossan Polis, are they?

She said if the motor didn't hurry up, the polis would come and take us away in the van.

Then a big yell went up from everybody.

–Here it comes!

–It's the matchbox!

I asked Annie what was the matchbox.

–That's the wee one. There's another one, the big one . . . That's the green Morris, it's got celluloid windows in the canvas sides but you can't see out of the matchbox unless you look under the flaps.

Then I lost their hands as everybody started to punch and fight and kick to get up the back step into the bus and I managed to hold on to Lizzie Boyle's dress and was pulled through the crowd.

I went up the back steps and into the far corner of the bus without my feet touching the ground. I couldn't see my sister or Lizzie.

–Annie! Annie!

–I'm over here Patrick, it's all right just stay where you are!

I heard the man turning the handle then the engine started and the matchbox drove away and a cheer went up. I was in a corner with a knee in my back and my nose stuck up against the side and someone pressing down my head and I had to stay like this all the way into Saltcoats till the motor stopped outside the gates of Saint Mary's School.

A man dressed like a polisman was standing at a big iron gate ringing a bell and Annie said that was the janitor, we'd better run because if you don't get in the gate before the bell stops ringing he clinks your ear as you run past. I looked up at him and his eyes gleamed down at me over his beard like a monster's as we got past him then Annie and Lizzie left me in a big porch with some other wee weans and they said they'd see me at dinner time. There was a great big woman in glasses with black rims round them and brown polished shoes with flaps over the laces the same as the golfers wear.

–I'm Miss O'Brien, children. Just get into a line and march into the class behind all these other children.

These other children were laughing but we were all girning. She made us tell her our names, one after the other.

–Patrick O'Connor, nine Harbour Place, Ardrossan, Ayrshire, Scotland.

–I just want your names.

She wrote them down in a book and said it was the register. We sat down on chairs with a little bit of wood in front of them and she said

–Hands up when I call out your names.

I could hardly stop wingeing and crying because I knew I wouldn't hear m'mammy's voice calling to me for my dinner and after a while a bell rang.

–Is that hometime?

–No, it's only playtime.

At dinner time I had my rolls in a corner by the hot pipes with Lizzie and Annie and when the bell rang to go back I wanted to go with them and they had to drag me back to the class and Miss O'Brien pulled me in the door. I began to kick the iron rails of my seat and she said to stop that at once. Then she pointed to a board with a stick and said to the class

–Say after me : I, T, it! I, T, it!

Over and over again we went

–I, T, it! I, T, it!

as if we were singing a song.

I got fed up and when we came to the end of another I, T, it, I said

–I, T, it, the baby's tit!

I, T, it, the baby's tit!

and she brought me out to the front of the class and made me stand in a corner facing the wall.

A bell rang and I rushed out with the others.

–Is this hometime?

–No, only playtime.

I was bursting to pee since dinner time and could hardly hold it in, standing in the corner. Two boys said they'd show me where the closet was. We went across a playground through a porch out a door across another playground covered in black cinders to a closet in the far corner made of shiny brown bricks. A crowd of boys in the door were struggling to get in. And those at the front were trying to get out and they were all shouting blue murder. I was pushed to the front but I turned and tried to get back out again because two big boys were scooting pee at the crowd and keeping them from coming through the door. Their teapots were full up and swelling with pee and they had the ends squeezed up with their fingers and they would let it out sometimes and it would scoosh over everybody like a hose pipe. They scooted it over the boys till their teapots were empty then everybody rushed forward to get a pee and I was at the back again. I was afraid to go in because they all started scooting pee at each other and it was like the fire migade and I was bursting.

Then the bell rang and they all came running out and I had to duke round a corner to get out of the way. They all disappeared and the closet was empty so I went in and had a pee by myself and it took me a long time. But when I finished and turned round there were a lot of boys sitting looking at me. They were moaning and their eyes were popping out of their heads and there was a terrible smell, even worse than our closet in the backyard. They were all sitting along a plank and there was water running along behind them like the Galloway Burn with lumps of number two floating in it and caramel papers.

When I got out the bell had stopped ringing and the janitor saw me and I started running and he came at me holding the bell and I said to myself he's going to hit me with that big brass bell and I ran for my life and he ran after me and when I got to the class the teacher took me by the ear and stood me in the corner again.

I had a frame in front of me with coloured balls on it and

I had to count them. I was plunking them along the wire like bools from one end to the other when the bell rang.

–Is that hometime?

–No, only another playtime.

I went out into a corner of the hard playground in front of the porch. A lot of boys and lassies were standing around in a ring holding hands and singing

–Water, water, water
Growing up so high,
We are all maidens
And we must die!
Except Maria Taylor,
The eldest of them all.
She can dance and she can sing
And she can knock the wall down.
Try, try, try again,
Turn your backs to the wall again!

Then they all turned their backs and faced out. Somebody else went into the middle and they sang

–Except Billy Toner,
The eldest of them all!

Then they caught me and put me in the middle and joined hands and danced around singing

–Except Patrick O'Connor,
The eldest of them all!

But when they turned their backs I duked under their arms and ran out because that's a lassie's game.

I wished I was still in the ring when I found myself out in the middle of this playground with all the windows looking down on it. Big red knees rushed at me. Tackety boots were ringing and sliding on the flagstones. Big boys with their noses running and their shirts hanging out ran at me. I could hear them panting for breath and the thumps of their fists smashing into each other's ribs. It was like running through the Plantation Woods only this time I was standing still and the trees were running at me.

I duked out and in a few times and I was turning to get back to the ring in the corner of the playground when a big knee caught me in the back and the flagstones came up to meet my face like a door closing. I saw stars like in the comic cuts when someone goes bonk! and hits the man on the head with a big club only they were not like written stars but more like fireworks of different colours then everything went blank.

I sort of dreamt that I was being carried up a stair like a dead soldier and then a nurse was bathing my face because I was wounded and then she said

–Now, sit up son.

I sat up. She said

–You were knocked out in the playground and you're to sit quietly for a while.

She gave me a cup of cocoa.

I thought only boxers got knocked out. I heard my daddy saying about knock-outs. He knew a boxer called Tommy Milligan. I said to myself I was a boxer and I had just been knocked out.

The nurse took me back to the class and Miss O'Brien took me by the hand and patted my head and gave me a sweetie and said

–Just you sit quietly in the corner and look at this book, Patrick.

And when a boy or a lassie came up to me I said I got knocked out. I got knocked out. I got knocked out.

8

The postman shouted up the stairs
–Post for O'Connor!
He never comes up the stairs because of the dirt all over them and you have to go down to Boyle's landing to get the post. Mammy said to run down it might be a parcel and I went down but it was only a letter.

–We'd better get the backyard done, you're going to help me my wee son.

That's what I had come straight home from school for, because it was Friday, m'mammy's turn to do the backyard. Every week is somebody's turn, the McGraws, the Boyles, the Brannifs and down in the close, the Taylors and the Hasties.

She put an apron around her, made from a flour bag and a pair of m'daddy's old working boots with his thick grey woollen socks on to fill them up. I had on the old wellingtons that lie under the set-in bed beside m'daddy's old pipes and his empty beer bottles. She took the black pail and I carried the hard brush over my shoulder like a rifle and we went down the stairs. First, mammy had to clear out the drain under the spicket with a long bit of wire before we could get to it because it was all stapped up with vegetables and tea leaves and slops and dirt. Sarah Brannif was leaning out of the window and mammy shouted up

–Is that not a terrible mess, the dirt of some people would sicken a pig.

–Aye, is that not a terrible mess, Missus O'Connor, sure you could talk till you were blue in the face but some people would never be clean.

–Aye, that's right, the dirt is ground into them, so it is.

–They're too bloody lazy to walk to the bucket, they just empty their dirty slops over the stairs.

–Look, I'm up to my ankles in it Sarah!

–It's enough to make you speak to the Factor, so it is Missus O'Connor.

–Aye, and what will he do for you? Sure they won't even mend our roof which is leaking and the fire needs mending and you can't close one of the windows.

Then it all started to gurgle and it ran away leaving a condensed milk tin and tea leaves and porridge and cabbage stalks and a baby's sock and a boy's belt with a snake clasp. It was shovelled up and put in the rubbish bucket then I filled the black pail with water and sloshed away the rest of the dirt. My job was to keep filling the black pail with water and sloshing it over the bricks while mammy brushed them with the hard brush. The worst part was at the top round by the two closets. There is one closet for the three families on our side and one for the three on the other side and the floors of both were covered in number two and it was running down the side of the crock and all over the backyard outside, right down to the corner of the wash-house. Mammy had her sleeves rolled up and she stood at the corner of the wash-house and took the pails of water from me as I ran up and down to the spicket and sloshed them in the closet door and scrubbed hard with the brush and when she was finished the sweat was running down her face but the closets were spotless and smelling of disinfectant.

–It would break your heart so it would for it will be as bad as ever by the morning but you have to try to keep the place clean.

I felt that I wanted to put my arms round her and say never mind, mammy, like Mary used to do with me.

Then we washed our hands under the spicket and went back up the stairs to the attic.

–That's a good wee boy for helping your mammy . . . And that's all the work done . . . So run across to Murchie's the bakers and get a rhubarb tart and one for yourself and I'll make a wee cup of tea before the rest comes in.

I had to balance the paper bags in my hands with the tarts sitting up the right way because the juice would run out of the rhubarb one but I had a pineapple tart, they are the best. There is yellow icing on top and underneath is soft, white cream and then a layer of pineapple and they are great.

We sat at the table and ate the tarts. Mammy had taken the flour bag off and m'daddy's old boots and put on black strapped shoes and a clean white blouse with a brooch on the front. She sighed and said

–Well that's all the work done then, thank God!

The place had a nice smell of soap and Brasso. The oil-cloth was scrubbed clean and still had damp patches on it and it was covered with newspapers at the door for their dirty feet coming in. The windows were cleaned, the wee table sitting in front with a fresh white pail of drinking water underneath. The orange boxes where the blackening brushes are kept had clean curtains in front of them. The big bed was made and the brass knobs polished. The delf was hanging along the dresser. Around the mantelpiece the brass plate tacked on to it was shining along with the candlesticks above and the clock ticking away beside them. There was a brass rod through the handles of the smokeboard over the fire and that was polished too. The hob and fender had been done with emery cloth, the grate blackleaded and the hearth whitened with stooky. The set-in bed had clean curtains closed over it so that it was just like another wee room but you wouldn't get very far if you tried to go in, there was a big wooden board along the side of the bed just behind the curtains.

I sometimes crawl underneath to hide behind the washing bin and the clothes basket among the empty beer bottles and you can listen to all the voices around the fire and look up at the straw mattress bulging through the wooden slats but you have to watch because there is some fluff and dust in there and sometimes a cockroach comes out.

All the wee bits of coal had been swept into the coal house and the black pail had disinfectant in it and had been put behind the door and a space left so that if you wanted a pee you could go in and close the door behind you and do it. It made a noise like the rain on the roof of the wash-house.

Next door the McGraws were all shouting and bumping then they began to sing

–Granny Noper, Granny Noper,
My cup's full an' Granny Noper!
May the Lord save me,
I'm as happy as can be.
My cup's full 'an Granny Noper!

I said

–Mammy, who's Granny Noper?

She made a face and said

–Ah, them an' their oul' heathen songs, don't listen to them, don't listen to them!

–Can we go to the pictures tonight?

She said that reminded her and turned a vase upside down and a half-a-crown dropped out and she put it in a book and said that was the rent and put it behind the picture of a man with thorns around his heart that hangs beside the photo of wee Dennis that died in convulsions when he was a baby before I was born.

–That's your wee brother that you never saw, he was a lovely wee boy, so he was, my wee Dennis.

–Was he as nice as me?

She laughed.

–Oh, well no, sure you're the apple of your daddy's eye, so you are!

–Who's the beardie with the holly around his heart, is that another brother that I never saw?

–Oh!

She put her hands up to her mouth.

–Hush! That's the Sacred Heart, he'll hear what you're saying!

I looked up at the picture again.

–He doesn't look as if he's listening, mammy.

–Yes, all right. We'll go to the pictures tonight.

9

After the supper I had to have my face washed again then mammy and John and Annie and I went away to the pictures.
Mammy said
–Will you be all right, Dan?
as she went out the door.
—Aye, I've got the oul' pipe, I'll be all right.
Coming out the close I saw Alec Taylor playing at bools in the gutter and he looked up and asked me where I was going. I said I was getting to the pictures and he said he had been there, it was good, *Felix the Cat*. We stopped at Isa Robertson's and mammy sent Annie in for tuppence worth of peppermint creams. Annie said
–I don't like going in for them mammy, it's very high class and they won't give you tuppence worth.
–Go you on in. And get Isa, not the other one. And go over to the side where no-one will see or hear what you're saying or doing and she'll give you tuppence worth of peppermint creams, sure sometimes she puts in a couple of odd caramels as well.
–I don't like doing it, mammy, tell John to do it.
John said
–That's great. I've got to go down and get a pail of water when it's snowing or raining and I'm slipping on the stone steps with the frost and I've got to empty the black pail and I'm out all day looking for work and when I come home there's no tea left for me and she won't go in and get the sweeties.
My mammy said to Annie
–Go on you in out a' this or I'll turn another pin in your nose, my lady,
and shoved her into the shop.

As we went across the street we had to stop to let Mick Kelly's motor get past, not the match box but the green Morris, it was bringing people in from Saltcoats. I rubbed my nose and tried to think what it would be like to have a pin turned in it then we were outside the Princes Picture House at the corner of Hill Street and Princes Street.

We went through the doors past big coloured pictures up on the wall with horses and men dressed like they were in a band and big lassies, very high class like Isa Robertson or the girl with red lips behind the counter in Murchie's the baker. There was a wee pigeon-hole and a girl looking out of it with tickets hanging down in front of her eyes like streamers and over the top it said SEATS. THREEPENCE, SIXPENCE, NINEPENCE AND A SHILLING. M'mammy was whispering something to John and dunting him in the ribs and he was squavering about and his face was getting red. Every time he opened his mouth to speak, mammy would give him another dunt in the ribs and say

–Sh, out a' that wi' ye! Go on you on now or I'll tell your father when we get home!

and her voice dropped and she whispered again. Then John took a sixpence from her hand and went up to the pigeon-hole and I heard him saying two threepennies as mammy took me by the hand up the stair at the side where we waited by the pipes, they were turned off.

When John came up the stair his face was redder and mammy took two tickets from his hand. Then she said

–Now Annie you go behind me, and Patrick, you behind Annie and stay like that till we get past the man.

Then she opened a door and a man said

–Good evening, Missus O'Connor and how's Dan?

I was holding on to the buttons at the back of Annie's coat and she kept putting her hand behind and trying to knock mine away but I would just put it up again. My mammy was saying

–Hullo, Sanny, sure he's fine, aye he's at home tonight with the oul' pipe.

They went on talking away and mammy was giggling and

all the time Annie was sliding me round slowly and m'mammy was sliding her round slowly. John was standing close beside mammy where she had him in a grip and she was talking away to the man, twenty to the dozen. When we had our backs to the screen, all the people were looking at us from their seats and pointing. Annie took my hand and whispered to come on and she led me down the passage to a door marked EXIT where we waited beside big velvet curtains.

Then John came down with m'mammy and she said

–Come on you's, come on you's childher

and led us into the seats. I went up beside the pipes next to John. His face had got redder and mammy was saying to him

–Hould your whisht and never you mind. Sure I know Sanny McKenzie and Sanny McKenzie knows me and he knows your father well and he always lets the weans slip past. Haven't I been coming here this many's a year? Did you think I was going down to the threepenny seats? I wouldn't go down there for love nor money, I'll sit here in the sixpennies and sure Sanny doesn't pay any attention at all. Sanny's all right, he's one of the best so he is. You'd never find me going down to the threepennies, down among all the roughs of the Fenian Row and Kilmahew Street and them all with the scabs on their heads and the snotters running from their nose!

All the weans were in the front two rows and they were most of them making so much noise you could hardly hear the piano jingling. And they kept throwing things at the back of the man playing it at the side of the screen, trying to hit him on the back of the neck. He had to keep jumping up from his stool and telling them off. Sanny McKenzie came rushing down shouting

–Keep quiet! Keep quiet!

I won't tell you again!

Get off the back of that seat, Ballantyne!

I'll tell your faither, McGinn! I'll see him the morra!

Everything went quiet suddenly and Sanny standing with his finger pointing. The man playing the piano looked round at him then began to play the tune that the Pipe Band marches to and Sanny marched back up the passage and as he passed us he smiled at my mammy and she said

–That's right Sanny, you're the boy to keep them in order!

After a wee while the weans began stamping their feet to the tune of the piano and then everybody began joining in until it seemed the whole picture house was doing it and it sounded like the Territorials marching across the railway crossing. And all you could see were papers being flung across from one seat to the other then the man banged the keys of the piano and stopped playing and jumped up and all the feet stopped with him. Sanny McKenzie came rushing down again and shouted

–The next wan to make that row will get flung oot!

Then Big Alec Ballantyne who lives over our wall blew a raspberry as Sanny was turning to go back. He stopped, walked slowly back down then suddenly dived into the second row and came out holding Big Alec by the ear. He said

–Do you think I didn't see you? I know you, Ballantyne, but you're oot noo!

He led him all the way up the passage by the ear with the man at the piano playing the tune that he plays when the sheriff chases the bad yins and everybody laughing and shouting and standing up on their seats to see him. He got him to the door marked EXIT and shoved him out saying

–Don't come back again!

Then he turned.

–You can all get doon off your seats an' keep quiet. I'm watching you, McGinn!

It was quiet for a wee while then they were all starting to fight again and two of the McGinns were thumping each other and Annie said

–Mammy, somebody's got hold of my leg under the seat.

The McGinns fell off their seat on to the floor and one of them was hitting the other one's head against the pipes and everybody was getting up on their seat again and throwing paper when the curtain that has all the coloured bits on it—they're advertisements, John told me—COWAN'S CLEANSER AND A.1 SOAP POWDERS and IRON BRU LEMONADE and COYLE'S FISH RESTAURANT and MURCHIE'S BAKERS GROCERS AND HIGH-CLASS TEA ROOMS and THE BEST OF THE BREWIN' MC EWAN and THE CASINO PICTURE HOUSE SALT-COATS UNDER THE DIRECTION OF HARRY KEMP and BEST CUTS AND A SQUARE DEAL FROM CHARLIE LOTHIAN BUTCHERS AND PURVEYORS and GET YOUR OWN BACK AT THE CO-OPERATIVE WHOLESALE SOCIETY and H.P. SAUCE and CASTLEBANK CLEANERS AND DYERS and HERE WE GO KERR AND CO. and THE ARDROSSAN AND SALTCOATS HERALD—started to go up and it got a bit quieter. The piano stopped playing, the lights went out and everybody gave a big cheer. The TOPICAL BUDGET came on and the piano played a quick tune.

Up on the screen some lassies dressed funny pushed a wee square cart on four wheels down the shore then dived into the waves with all their clothes on—a man with big deep wrinkles on his face, wearing a black soft felt hat and a fur collar like m'mammy's got for Sundays came out of a bank and stood looking at us as if he was going to cry—a shipyard and the keel of a big boat on the slips and a lot of shipyard men bobbing up and down and shaking their fists—a warship coming into a harbour with flags all over it—rolls of paper going round on wheels—Flowers—a big chimley smoking—a band playing then soldiers marching along with rifles over their shoulders and big black twirly moustaches, but they were wearing white frilly skirts like lassies wear at their first communion, and the whole picture house was roaring and laughing at them. Annie and John and I were bursting our sides, and we couldn't stop when Felix the Cat came on. He is a great cat, not a tiger like Toby but a black one. You can hit him with a great big hammer but he just bounces up again like he was made of rubber, you get a great laugh. Then it was the COMING ATTRACTIONS. Somebody began to kick the EXIT door and shout through the keyhole

–Aw, mah maw's big tumshie! Hullaw! Mah ma's big tumshie!

Then they kicked the door again and ran away. STUPENDOUS ATTRACTION NEXT MONDAY TUESDAY AND WEDNESDAY. The piano played the kind of music when something is going to happen. TEN NIGHTS IN A BAR-ROOM ! ! ! with WILLIAM FARNUM. They showed his photo and he looked like Peter Milne the coalman after he's washed his face, his eyes were still black. ALSO THE TOPICAL BUDGET. FELIX THE CAT. THE NEXT INSTALMENT OF THE EXCITING SERIAL : LEATHERSTOCKING. INTEREST AND ANOTHER LUCKY DRAW FOR SUPERIOR PRIZES ! ! !

Then it was the continued picture THE COVERED WAGON. This week AMBUSH AT CRAZY CREEK. The piano played away at the same note over and over again. LEATHERSTOCKING is on Monday, Tuesday and Wednesday, and THE COVERED WAGON is on Thursday, Friday and Saturday.

We have wagons that go past the window down in the shunting yard and sometimes they are covered with oilskins like m'daddy when it's raining, but I couldn't see any in this picture although it was called The Covered Wagon. I couldn't see one anywhere, and I asked John where the covered wagon was and he said he'd never been able to find it himself.

When that ended the lights went up again and everybody began to murmur and take out their half-tickets and look at the number. Sanny McKenzie came walking down the passage with a tin box in his hand and everybody cheered again. He went in a door then came out on the stage with the box in his hand.

–Now, I want a nice little girl from the audience to come up on the stage and pick the lucky numbers.

A lot of wee lassies put their hands up.

–That wee girl with the red hair, no you, no no, no you hen, no, that wee girl there, no, the other one. . . .

Mammy said to Annie to stand up, he was pointing at her and she stood up.

–Aye, that's right, you hen.

Mammy gave her a push and she went out of the row, down to the front through a door and came out on the stage in front of the screen and stood beside Sanny. She had that look on her face that she has when she eats something that makes her sick or when she smells someone doing number two.

–I'm going to ask this little girl to pick a number for the first prize, a lovely leatherette armchair that will go beside your fire.

He held the box down to Annie. She put her hand in and drew out a half-ticket. Sanny took it from her and said

–Number nought nought nine six three three. Number nought nought nine six three three, for the lovely leatherette armchair!

Mammy said

–Look at your ticket, go on you John!

Then she looked at her own.

–Jesus, Mary and Joseph, that's my number!

Everybody turned round and looked at her and she was standing up and shouting

–Here Sanny, over here Sanny, it's my number, I've got it here!

Sanny said to come down to the front with the ticket and give her name and address and collect the prize tomorrow. So she shoved John out and he went down then came back with Annie and she had a box of caramels for going up on the stage but she still looked as if she was smelling something.

–And that's all, ladies and gentlemen, there'll be another lucky draw next Friday night!

The lights went out again and then it was the big picture. Somebody came and kicked the door again.

–Your pictures are rotten!

You get your prizes from the pawn!

Awa' mah ma's big tumshie!

GIGANTIC. AN EPIC OF THE SEA! the piano played the tune when something is going to happen then this great big boat sailed on to the screen with all its port holes lit up, hundreds and hundreds of them—A man with a skippit bunnet—he's a captain, John said—looked at this girl who had shiny eyes and shiny lips and spiky eyelashes—the piano played the tune when they are going to kiss—then they kissed and their eyes twinkled like the lights of Ayr and you could see the moon over their shoulder and everybody began to giggle and blow raspberries and mammy said she didn't like all this slabbering and they kissed again and everybody booed. Then a man was lying on a bed and a priest was sitting beside him with that scarf hanging around his neck and the big girl was crying then you saw an iceberg coming and everybody in the pictures went quiet. Then somebody began to kick the door again.

–Missus McDougal, your house is on fire!

Mister McCanse, stinking fish!

Hullaw, mah maw's big tumshie!

This time Sanny was hiding behind the velvet curtains and he opened the door quick and jumped out. Then we heard feet scuffling and running away and a boy shouted

–I'll get mah faither to you!

–I'll kick your arses if you come back again!

Sanny closed the door again and the man on the screen began to roll his head from side to side on the pillow and the piano played a sad tune and m'mammy got her hankie out and began to rub her eyes. Then somebody rolled an empty bottle from the back right to the front. It went rattling over the wooden floor with a kick here and there to help it on its way and everybody burst out laughing.

Then this iceberg began to get nearer and nearer and nearer—the bow of the boat went into it and you could see all the plates falling off the tables—people who were dancing began sliding along the floor and falling down, then others were in rowing boats—they're lifeboats, John told me—and a lot jumped into the water—a sailor with braid on his cap had a gun in his hand and he was pointing it at a crowd—the boat began to capsize and all the people slid down the decks—the propellers went up in the air and the piano played the tune when the boat's going down.

Then it was THE END and I got very sleepy.

–Give me a carry, John, g'on, give me a carry.

M'mammy said

–Give the wee soul a carry.

–Ach, all right.

He picked me up and carried me out among all the crowd, kicking and fighting to get out, and we crossed Princes Street and I fell asleep and dreamt we were going around the Union Bank of Scotland on the way home, and Letty Taylor was looking at me with spiky eyelashes as the moon shone over the Church of the Nazarene.

10

Nobody goes to school on Saturdays and the shipyard men only work till twelve o'clock, and even the Belfast Boat men who work all the time get away early and the dockers at the iron ore and Mister McAteer who works on the Co-operative coal in the Railway Yard and Sam Clark the patrolman in the Shell-Mex and anybody else, they all finish when the horns blow at twelve o'clock.

I could hear some wee boys down in the Big Pen singing

–*Micky Kelly burst his belly*
O'er the heid o' a pot o' jelly!
Micky Kelly burst his belly
O'er the heid o' a pot o' jelly!

Then the man came round who shouts

–Nice pork ribs!
Pork ribs and hocks!

He's got a funny barrow with two wheels at the back and one at the front and it's like a hut on wheels with a wee wooden door, and if anybody wants any meat he pulls out a wooden board and chops the meat with a great big hatchet. M'mammy said she thought she'd get some ribs to make stew for you get them cheap from the man with the wee barrow.

–Nice pork ribs!
Pork ribs and hocks!

He sang it like a funny song with not much tune to it. I said

–Can I come down to the street with you, mammy, and stay out and play for a wee while?

–Yes, but don't go too far away, and you watch for your daddy coming home and come in and get your dinner.

I stood at the wee barrow for a while watching the man chopping the ribs with his hatchet, then m'mammy put some in her apron and went upstairs. There was a big crowd of boys and lassies and they were playing Roon the Wee World. It's a race between two of the best racers. They leave the same spot, but one goes one way and one the other, down Harbour Place, Bute Place, Princes Street, Harbour Street, then back to Harbour Place again. I asked if I could get a game, and Alec Taylor said

–Do you want to race roon the wee world?

–I'll race you, I can beat you!

Everybody shouted

–Patrick O'Connor's going to race Alec Taylor!
Alec Taylor's going to race Patrick O'Connor!

They all cheered, then the man sang his song again.

–Nice pork ribs! Pork ribs and hocks!

He pushed his barrow through us all and away further up the street. Sailor McFarlane was smoking his pipe and looking at us all with his eyes crinkled, and Missus Boyce was leaning out of her top window and shouting down to Robert Cook's mother.

–I hear the San Umberto's coming in. That's the boat your man's on, is it no?

Missus Cook shouted back

–Aye, that's right, Missus Boyce, an' it's supposed to be due in this week-end.

I said to Robert Cook

–Is the San Umberto bigger than the Glen Sannox?

–Aye.

–Is it bigger than the King Orry?

–Aye, it beats the lot of them, it's a tanker!

Then all the lassies shouted to hurry up with the race. Robert Taylor had a piece of chalk and he drew a line across the street outside the Big Pen. That was the winning post. George Hall, a big boy, said he'd be the referee. We stood with our backs to each other, me facing down towards the harbour where you could see the funnel of a coal boat sticking up over the jail, and Alec up towards the Church of the Nazarene and the Railway Wall at the corner of Bute Place.

George Hall lifted his hand and said he'd count up to three then go.

–One!
Two!
Three!
Go!

I pushed away as quickly as I could and began to run away from the Big Pen past Missus Smith's close—Tuohy's second-hand shop on the other side—Murchie's Bakehouse—I had to dodge over to the other side of the street to Nicol's Bar as the baker's cart was coming out—then I turned the corner into Harbour Street past the green closets where the men sometimes leave empty beer bottles that you could get a penny on—past the seats where the old men sit with their clay pipes, spitting on the stones—down past the Town Hall —E. Currie's corner at the Town Cross with the signpost in the middle, one arm pointing up Glasgow Street, another to Ardrossan Harbour, another South Beach and Saltcoats and the other Montgomerie Street and the North shore. I turned into Princes Street—Crawford's Newspaper Shop—Murchie's the Grocers, the smell of roasting coffee as I went past—Murchie's Pastry Shop, the girl with red lips was smiling through the window and this made me slow down a bit—The National Bank of Scotland—Allison's, Ladies' and Gentlemen's Outfitters—Isa Robertson's—I looked across to the Picture House and the bill was a man with a gun on a horse and he was looking right across the street at me—Arthur Guthrie and Sons' Bookshop—Cameron's the Grocer —Then Alec Taylor came running towards me and we gave each other a dunt as we went past and I shouted I was winning and he shouted back, no I wasn't, and I ran even harder—Jarvie's Pub with barrels for windows—round the corner at the Union Bank of Scotland, across from the Commercial Hotel where the dog runs out at you, but it wasn't there this time—into Bute Place with the Church of the Nazarene facing me at the end—past the Good Templar's Hall, across from Missus McAteer's house—round Tomelty's corner into Harbour Place again—then a big cheer went up from all the boys and lassies and I couldn't see Alec Taylor then he suddenly came out of Murchie's Bakehouse

Yard, he'd taken a short cut through the close and I put on my highest speed till I was nearly bursting and reached the Big Pen just as Alec reached Tuohy's Shop and I crossed the line before he got to it and I won.

The boys clapped me on the back and the lassies turned away and wouldn't look at me and giggled. Then they were asking who was going to race next and George Hall said we would choose for it. All the boys lined up against the wall except the two who had raced and George went

–*Eachy peachy peary plum*
Out goes my chum.
My chum's not well,
Out goes mysel'!

The one that his finger rested on last stood out until there were only two left and they had to race.

I wandered away and even though I beat Alec Taylor he came with me up to the corner of Bute Place and we climbed on to the railings of the Church of the Nazarene and right along to the end at the Railway wall and we tried to climb up on that but it was too high. Then we heard a train coming, it was on the line nearest the wall and we were able to pull ourselves up by the hands to see over and this engine came along, it was a pug, the kind that pulls wagons with only a wee place behind the wagon for coal and there was a man looking out of the cabin and he laughed at us and waved his hand and we shouted

–Hi, mister, gi'es a run in your train!

And he was still looking back at us as the engine went behind Missus McAteer's backyard and up past the Commercial Hotel just before you get to the Station Gates. Then the wagons started coming past. N.B., a long slanty white line across the front—C.W.S., the line slanting the other way—G.E.C.—Paddy—Belfast Boat written in chalk—FYFFE'S BANANAS, pink coloured with doors in them—tin wagons filled with white stooky that my mammy does the hearth with—Big long wagons filled with scrap iron, sometimes you can get a roller skate, one boy got a real cowboy's gun you could hardly lift but it was all rusty—then the wagons all started clinking and stopped, then they moved back the other way a bit then they stopped again and Alec Taylor shouted

–The gates are shut!

We climbed down from the wall and jumped down off the railings and looked up towards Princes Street.

Mick Kelly's green Morris was stopped at the gates and people were looking through the celluloid. The Co-operative baker's cart came up and stopped behind it with wee Mister Williamson sitting on the top like a stage coach driver. Then up behind him came Sanny Reid the milkman with the cans clanking hung at the back of the cart to catch the dreeps from the big milk cans that have polished brass bands around them. There were yellow rims round the cart wheels and yellow designs on the wooden strips around the cart. Across the back it said MONTFODE DAIRY and all the brass was glinting and Sanny Reid wore a long light brown milkman's coat and leather gaiters and trousers like cowboy's. M'daddy says he always has a word for everybody. Two big bugs from up the North Shore came behind in their pony and trap. The pony was a beezer, it had black leather harness with bells at the top. Then Wee Bradley, the vegetable man. The horses did a dung on the street while they waited for the gates to open then Joseph Cook came running round the Union Bank of Scotland corner in the wee world race. His face was red from running hard and Alec and I shouted

–Come on Josie!

Come on Josie!

We looked up the other way and we couldn't see anybody coming around Harbour Street corner so we shouted again

–You're winning!

We canny see him yet!

Then the big dog came out of the Commercial Hotel and ran straight for Joseph Cook, barking and snarling and Josie turned and ran back the other way as fast as he could with the dog after him and did the disappearing trick round the corner. So we ran up to the station gates to get there before they started to open for you can get a swing on them.

We just got on to the gates as the last wagon of the train was going underneath the station bridge and I had to shove Alec Taylor along the gate to make room for me to get on. Then the man in the signal box with the bands on his shirtsleeves came over to the window and looked out then got hold of the big double wooden wheel by the handle sticking out of the side and began turning it. And we shouted hullaw, hullaw and had to hold on tight as the gates began to open with a rush, then they would slow down, then they would rush again. We jumped off when they were open full and ran round to outside the Commercial Hotel Bar again before the carts would start to come through. Alec Taylor said

–There's your faither.

–Where?

–Coming out of Missus Rae's.

I looked across at the corner of Hill Street and Princes Street to Mary Barbour's Toy Shop and Miss Rutherford's Fruit Shop and m'daddy was coming out of the RAILWAY BAR next door. He stopped on the pavement outside and two other big men were talking to him and they all had beery bottles sticking out of their jacket pockets. Then he turned and stepped off the pavement and came across Princes Street with his two hands stuck in the front pockets of his moleskin trousers, his jacket thrown open and the cap at the back of his head. He stepped back to let the Co-operative coal cart go past, the driver was standing up and whipping the horse and it was galloping and the man shouted

–How're ye, Dan!

–Not so bad at all, Joe!

Then the cart was past and he came on across the street again.

–I'm away to m'daddy, Alec.

–Aye, I think I'll go and get a piece of bread and jeely, are you coming out after your dinner?

I said aye and ran across to the lamp post at the corner of the Union Bank of Scotland. I climbed up on the bottom bit of the lamp post. You put one foot on the bit that sticks out at one corner, you hang on to the post and bring your other foot between your left foot and the lamp post and put it on the next corner then you put your left foot over the right on to the next corner and you go right round the lamp post like that, hanging away out with one arm stuck out like the chair-a-planes at the fair and you see how fast you can go round without tripping and falling off. When you get off you stand still and the world goes round and it makes you stagger or you'll fall down and then my daddy was bending down and looking at me and he said

–*Brown eyes why are you blue?* Ha-ha! *Brown eyes why are you blue?*

I said

–Gi'es a penny, daddy, or gi'es a halfpenny
and if you haven't got a halfpenny a piece of bread will do and if you haven't got a piece of bread, God bless you.

He laughed.

–How's my wee fella? How's my wee man?
Brown eyes, why are you blue? Brown eyes should always be true!

He took hold of my hand.

–Come on my wee sonny mick and we'll go and get our dinner.

–Gi'es a halfpenny, daddy.

–You never know your luck, so you don't, no you never know your luck.

We went away down Bute Place for our dinner, me skipping alongside to keep up with him.

James McAteer was out at his coal house splitting sticks for the fire in his peaked bunnet. He's lucky, his coal house is outside the house along a bit from the wash house and he's bigger then me and his mammy lets him split the sticks out on the pavement. He looked over at me and waved and I waved back then a sheet blew across him for his mammy had her washing out to dry on a line tied to his roof and the other end tied to the lamp post outside the Church of the Nazarene. The line goes across the street at the wee corner where the rubbish buckets are but we're not to play in and out the clothes hanging on the line because Missus McAteer comes out and chases us away.

I looked down the street and the boat behind the jail blew its horn and I said look to daddy and pulled his hand and he stopped and said what and I pointed at the black funnel of the boat moving slowly along behind the building.

–Aye, it's going out.

–Where is it going?

–It's going out to sea.

We turned into the close and my daddy stopped and put his hand in the pocket of his trousers and I heard money clinking and he said to wait till we would see, wait till we would see, he would see if he hadn't got something for the wee man. He looked down at me over his big moustache and I was looking up at him. Then he pulled his hand out of his pocket and said

–Shake hands, brother. You're a rogue and I'm another.

I shook hands with him and he pressed a halfpenny into my hand.

–What will you buy with that?

–A sooker.

–Will you give me a suck? . . . Don't tell anybody I gave you a halfpenny.

We went on up the stairs for our dinner.

We had fried links and beef ham with spice on it and m'mammy gave me a big piece of bread dipped in the pan on my plate, the white crust end that you can chew and not the black end. I got a wee bit of beef ham with my links but not much as we can only buy a quarter as it's very dear.

My daddy put his beery bottles under the set-in bed and washed his face and hands before eating and when he ate, the brass stud in his shirt went up and down on his adam's apple. M'mammy said

–Things are getting awful dear, I don't know how we're going to manage on one man's wage at all, at all. Patrick is growing up and he needs a new pair of trousers, the backsides are nearly out of the ones he's wearing and

Annie needs clothes and John needs clothes, sure he hasn't got a jacket to his back except the oul' one that you left off that is too big for him and as for the shoes and the boots, Patrick kicks all the boots off his feet in no time at all, it's a good job Auntie Annie is keeping Bridget in 'Derry or I don't know what we'd do.

Daddy said

–I'm only an oul' common five eight as the man said. Yis, I'm only an oul' common five eight and I only have a working man's wage, sure it wouldn't keep a fly . . .

–No, but you have enough money to buy your old beer.

–Ah, sure they're only a couple of wee dumps. They're only a couple of wee dumps, that's all they are. Small bottles that wouldn't fill a fly.

–I'll have to get Patrick a pair of trousers in Saltcoats.

–Aye, get him a good pair of cordy roys. You can't beat the oul' cordy roys.

–If only John could get a wee job to help out but sure they won't even give him any burroo money. They say he hasn't got enough stamps. And Annie has to be kept too, and she would eat you out of house and home . . .

–Yis, get him an oul' pair of cordy roys.

After we had our dinner I went up to John.

–Shake hands, brother. You're a rogue and I'm another.

John shook hands and said

–A rogue walks with two legs but I walk with four.

And I said

–And I canny tell you anymore,
Because my belly's getting sore!

Then the whole family was laughing and Annie couldn't stop and she was holding her belly and saying

–Oh, mammy, I can't stop,

and I said

–You'll burst your belly if you don't stop,

and that made her worse, and my mammy and daddy were laughing too, and m'daddy said

–I think you're a bit of an oul' comedian, Patrick, yis, I think you're a bit of an oul' comedian!

After dinner I looked out the window for a while and I saw the boat that was behind the jail come sailing out from behind the Fenian Row chimleys. It was a coaster with its funnel at the stern and it went away over towards Arran. Then I saw a wee puffer coming over from Ayr and a boat going in to Saltcoats quay. That's not a big harbour like ours, it only gets fishing boats and rowing boats and boats that take the visitors for a trip round the bay.

There was a knock on the door and m'mammy said

–That'll be the pearl. . . That'll be the pearl. Give me that book down off the mantelpiece.

John handed her a pasteboard book from behind the brass candlestick, then mammy opened the door and a wee man came in, very well dressed with a white collar and tie and a pen behind his ear. He had a coat with big pockets and he took out a thick book with elastic bands around it and opened it up and took some money from mammy and wrote something in the thick book and something in the pasteboard book.

–Nice day, Missus O'Connor.

–Aye, it's a fine day.

Then he said something about a policy, something to do with the polis and mammy said she was not going in for any more, just now, it was taking her all her time to make ends meet.

–Yes, you're right, Missus O'Connor, it's all you can do to earn your living today. . . . Good day, Missus O'Connor.

He snapped the elastics on his thick book and went out. Then we heard him knocking at the McGraws' door for a long time and there was no answer and mammy said he would never get any money out of them ones, so he wouldn't. It was all quiet, you couldn't hear a sound and m'daddy said

–Listen. . . . You wouldn't hear a pin drop, so you wouldn't. . . . And any other time you can hardly hear your ears.

Then the man got fed up and went away and when he was away out the close the McGraws began to move about again and the weans were soon out the door again and up and down the stairs yelling and fighting and crying.

I went over to m'mammy and pulled at her apron and said

–Mammy, can you not get the ends to meet? Mammy, why can you not get the ends to meet?

She pulled my face against her and rubbed my head and it was a great feeling and there was a nice kind of milky smell coming from her. I said

–Can I go out to play, mammy?

–All right, don't go too far away.

Annie said

–I want to go out too, mammy, I want to go to Morgans' close to play with Margit Morgan and Mary McFarlane.

–Aye, away you go, the pair of you.

John was sitting at the fire reading *The Rover*.

The McGraws began to fight next door, the man was shouting at the woman and John said to m'mammy that they were using bad language, and she said we were not to listen to them bloody heathens, then a plate smashed against the wall and you could hear them thumping each other. M'mammy said

–Away you two! Away out a this where you won't hear that!

We went away down the stairs and out the close. Annie went in Morgans' close and I went away round the corner into Bute Place to McAteer's wee shop to buy a sooker. Missus McAteer served me. She's got rosy cheeks. James McAteer was in the shop and I asked him if he was coming out and his mother said he was not to go too far away as she wanted him for some messages soon. He asked her if he could go down the Bath Rocks and she said all right but to remember what she had told him.

We went out the shop and down to beside his coal house. There were a lot of chips of wood lying outside and all the pavement was cracked. We climbed up on to his wash house window and shared the sooker. Peter Milne the coalman's horse had wandered away down the street by itself from the Commercial Hotel where he was in for a drink.

Old Paddy McNamee came around the corner from the station gates into Bute Place pulling a great big log along the street behind him and carrying a lot of old wood on his back. He is Robert and Joseph Cook's grandaddy and he lives through the Big Pen in the back room with Granny McNamee. He has got a long grey beard, a soft hat on his head and an old swallow-tailed coat that is a dark green colour. He goes down the shore and collects all the driftwood that is washed in, planks and logs. Then he breaks it all up through the Big Pen and sometimes he uses a chisel and a hammer on the logs with big knots in them. If you walk along behind him he chases you away. As he passed us we shouted

–Paddy McNamee!
Aul' Paddy McNamee!

Then he turned the corner into Harbour Place and all the weans saw him coming and they all got behind and began to march along singing

–Paddy McNamee wi' a hole in his knee!
Paddy McNamee wi' a hole in his knee!

He turned on them and shook his fist and shouted

–Get away a' that wi' ye!

We jumped down from the window sill and went with all the other weans and marched behind him singing

–Paddy McNamee wi' a hole in his knee!
Paddy McNamee wi' a hole in his knee!

Then some of them shouted

–Irish Paddy!
Irish Paddy!

This time he turned and ran after us and we all scattered.

–Come on, Patrick!

James said, and we turned and ran into Bute Place, and we didn't stop running till we got through the station gates into the Inches Road where we stopped under the Signal Box to get our breaths back.

There was a train coming, so I said would we go up the Station Bridge and climb up on the window and watch it going underneath. You can see into the wagons and into the cabin of the engine as the train goes through. The Station Bridge is covered in with glass windows and you're supposed to go over it when the gates are closed. It's got wooden stairs that lead on to the street and instead of going right over the bridge you can go down the stairs to platform number three in Ardrossan Town Station. James said

–No, come on down the Inches, we'll go over the Bath Rocks for a stiff yin, are you ready?

–I'll be ready in a wee while.

–Are you coming down for a big stiff yin, then?

–Aye, come on, we'll do a big stiff yin, come on.

We began to run down the Inches Road.

We passed ANDREW REID CONTRACTORS then we stopped at the billboards—DAVID ALLEN AND SON. For a while we spattered muck at them and made a moustache on the woman who was holding up a tin of Brasso, then we found a bit of a poster that was loose and we began to tear it off. Someone was rapping on a window and when we looked across the railway line it was James's big sister Alice shaking her fist at us out the back upstairs window, and James ran away at full speed with me at his heels. His red school bunnet fell off and I bent and picked it up without stopping like the cowboys do from their horses when they are being chased by the Indians or the bad yins, and they have to pick up the good lassie in a hurry on their horses without stopping.

I caught up with him at Mick Kelly's hut after duking through all the men standing outside backing horses with their papers and pencils and a bit of a fag stuck behind their ear. I gave him his bunnet, and he said he would get a row now when he went home, his big sister tells on him to his mammy. I said

–You should give her a kick on the leg with your tackety boots like I do. If my sister tells on me, I give her a good kick with my tackety boots.

–My mother would kill me!

–My mother wouldn't kill me or I'd get m'daddy to her. If your mother goes to hit you, you say you'll tell your daddy on her.

–She would hit my daddy as well!

We went along the rubbish dump, looking for clean bits

of paper, and James said we'd come down again and look for lux, you find great things sometimes, and then we slid down the dump for a while until our boots got filled with ashes. We had to sit on a rock and take our boots off to empty the ashes out, and then James said he'd got a big bit of clean paper, somebody had thrown away the *Weekly News*. We divided it between us and put a lump each in our pockets and made our way towards the Bath Rocks over the stones. Some were greeny where the sea had soaked into them, some were red stones like the Good Templar's Hall, and bits of broken delf in blue and white with designs on them, wee round black ones then big pieces all bricks stuck together with cement and big round white ones, and then we came to a long hard layer of dark brown flat rock that if you looked closely had all nails and nuts and bolts mixed up with the rock, and James said his daddy had told him that volcanoes made that.

–Where's the volcano, up the Cannon Hill?

–No.

–What's a volcano?

–It's a hill like the Cannon Hill but it's got a lum at the top that goes on fire sometimes and all the bricks come flying out.

The tide was going out and we got flat stones and played at skiffing them across the water for a while to see who could make the most skiffs before they sank, and I got a four then we got a four each. We made the wee round balls in the seaweed crack with our boots before crossing the big long line of it then we were on the green slippery stuff like soaken grass that you have to walk slowly on in case you fall into a puddle. Then we were nearly underneath the Bath Rocks, they were jutting up away over us like mountains and it was all quiet and there wasn't a sinner there except us. The Bath Rocks start off from behind the deserted old grey house that has the smiling lion made of stone sitting on top of the front gates and is all surrounded by weeds and bushes and is supposed to have ghosts in it. They run all the way across the stones into the sea then there is a gap before you come to the

Wee Cruiben Rock and then a bigger gap to the Big Cruiben Rock.

We had to put stepping stones down to get across a big puddle left by the tide going out. We wanted to get to a ledge that runs along the side of the rocks and after dodging some wee waves still coming in we came to a kind of big cut.

–Like a canyon,

James said.

–A cannon?

–No, a canyon. . . . Have you never heard of a cowboy riding down the canyon?

We turned up this and got away from the waves and suddenly it was all quiet like going into a cave and you could hear the wind whistling over the top and hear the sound of the sea as if it was miles away.

At the end of the cut there were some steps in the rock and some had the remains of old cement over them. James said

–That's the steps the smugglers went up with the loot on their backs.

–What smugglers?

–The Bath Rocks used to be a smuggler's lair where they landed off their boats at night and carried the loot up these steps.

–Did they?

–Yes.

–But did they?

–Yes.

He drew his finger across his throat and spat on the rocks. And the wind whistled louder and I turned like a captain and looked away out to sea past the Big Cruiben and I said to myself I bet there were pirates here as well.

He said

–Come on, we'd better find our places. You go that way and I'll go this way.

I climbed up and down the rocks leading round the corner to the South Beach until I found a wee place between two rocks with a shelf jutting out over it. I climbed back up but I couldn't see James then his head came up over a rock and I shouted

–Have you found a place?

–Yes, have you?

–Yes.

–I'll see you at the wee steps after.

Then I went back down to my place and cooried down in the corner and peeped out each way to see if anybody was coming and when I saw that nobody was coming I unbuttoned my trousers from their galluses and took them down. I crouched down on the wee stones. While crouching, I looked right along the shore, the white waves at the end, past the Galloway Burn where it comes out from the Plantation Woods under the bridge onto the sand to the Saltcoats Promenade, wee dots of people moving along and bigger blobs that would be carts or motors to the Pavilion and the Bathing Pond and the tower at the end of Saltcoats Quay sticking out. When I was finished I used the bit of the *Weekly News* that we got from the rubbish dump and threw it down.

I climbed back up over the rocks again and found James. He was just buttoning up his trousers and he said

–Are you finished?

–Yes.

–Did you do a stiff yin?

–Yes, I did a big stiff yin, did you?

–Aye, but we'll see who did the biggest!

We climbed over the rocks and had a look at mine. James said

–Mine is the biggest—Ye have to do a big stiff yin, Hamish—that's what my uncle says. Now we have to bury them.

So we gathered stones and covered them over and made two piles but the flies were still trying to get through the stones.

We climbed away over the rocks out to the end and sometimes we would find other wee crannies where other people had crouched down and the flies were buzzing all round and there was a rotten smell. The flies were light brown coloured and James said they were dung flies. We got to the end where the waves were splashing up on the rocks and the wind was blowing in from the sea and you could taste salt on your lips and the seagulls were whirling about and a motor boat was going across the bay and big white wullicks were sticking to the rocks we were standing on and James said

–You canny eat those, they are poison!

So we pulled them off and started throwing them to see if we could hit the Wee Cruiben Rock which was coming up out of the sea and the seagulls would rest on it sometimes before flying out again, but we couldn't throw them far enough.

A boat blew its horn in the harbour and we heard some riveters hammering in the shipyard but not as much as through the week and James said somebody must be working overtime. Then he burst out with

–Look, look, here comes the Herald Street Gang!

I looked over towards the Flute Band Hut and from behind were coming all these boys that you can see going over our wall for a shortcut to Herald Street which is the real name of the Fenian Row with torn trousers and some of them no boots on their feet and their noses running all the time and scabs on their heads and they were shouting like Indians and came jumping and rolling and falling down the rubbish dump and charging over the rocks towards us. James said

–I think they've seen us, we'd better run for it.

–What will they do if they catch us?

–They'll make a fire and tie us up then burn us but they'll torture us first.

–Oh, mammy, daddy!

–Never mind, we'll beat them yet. We'll go down the rocks and way round the back way. But I hope they haven't sent any of the gang round the other way to cut us off!

We climbed down over the rocks at full speed and started running along a cement ledge at the bottom of the sea wall, heading for the steps that lead up to Arran Place in front of the big English Church on the promenade. We were coming to the bit that goes up and down in humps before you turn the corner when James suddenly sprang back and put his finger up to his lips.

–Sh! There's two of them on the lookout over the wall at the top of the steps, we're cut off!

We could hear the shouts of the rest of the gang climbing up the other side of the Bath Rocks and they were getting nearer. I said

–Oh mammy, daddy, what will we do! They'll torture us and burn us and then they'll throw us into the sea!

I looked out towards the end of the sea and there was a big rock that you could hide behind. I said

–If we could crouch down and creep over through the rocks we could hide behind that big one.

–We couldn't get to it without being seen by the lookout. Then they would surround us with only the sea behind us and they would drive us into the sea and we would be drowned.

–Oh daddy, mammy, what will we do?

James was looking up the wall and after a while he said

–If we could climb up that wall and get over into the old garden at the back of the old grey house we could hide in there . . . Is it too high for you to climb?

–Yes.

–Will you give me a bunk up on to the first ledge at the top of the sea wall where the other wall starts then when I get up I'll pull you up.

So I bunked him up but he kept slipping down again as he was so heavy and all the time we could hear the gang getting nearer and nearer and singing

–Hullaw! Hullaw!
We are the Billy Boys.
Hullaw! Hullaw!
We are the Billy Boys!

This time I gave my biggest heave and James scrambled up on the ledge then I was left by myself with only the sighing of the sea behind me and the cries of the gang getting nearer and if I hadn't just done a stiff yin on the rocks I would have done it in my breeks. Then James pulled and pulled and I managed to get up on the ledge beside him. He said now he would climb up to the top of this wall and lie on the top and lean down to give me his hand and pull me up and he started climbing up and when he was nearly at the top he seemed a terrible long way away and when he leaned over to give me his hand I couldn't reach it and now I could hear the sound of their feet running along the ledge. So I started climbing up the wall myself and I was doing well and then James's hand was in front of me and I grabbed on to it and he stated pulling me up then there was a shout.

–There they are!

And I was straining to get on to the top of the wall and nearly pulling James off and then stones began to whistle round our ears but I was on the top at last and we both jumped down into the garden before any could hit us.

We ran for our lives through the old garden, over a broken down gate into the front and over some palings into Arran Place where all the people were walking up and down. And it was like in the pictures when the hero escapes from the natives and gets back to the good yin's town again and we laughed to each other and linked arms and jogged homewards.

11

We were glad when we turned into Bute Place and Harbour Place because that was our territory and the Herald Street Gang wouldn't touch us there.

–The real American apples,
Twelve for a tanner!

Tammy MacNamara's fruit cart was in the street.

–The great big juicy oranges,
Three and a half pounds for a tanner!

James said

–I'd better go in now and get the messages before the Co-operative shuts or my mother will be out looking for me. I'll see you again.

He ran down the street to his house. I turned into Harbour Place. One of Missus Cosgrove's hens had wandered away out of the run and come right out of the close into the street and when the weans all saw it they ran after it shouting hullaw and the hen turned and went squawking and half flying back in the close again with the weans after it and there was a terrible row down the close and then all the weans came running out again chased by Missus Cosgrove.

Tammy MacNamara had his hand up to the side of his mouth and he was shouting

–Ripe bananas, cheap bananas!
Ripe bananas, cheap bananas!
The real American apples,
Twelve for a tanner!

The cart was stopped in the street and the horse had its feed-bag on. Women and big lassies were buying fruit and putting it in their aprons and all the weans were pulling at them and asking for an apple. The McGraws were trying to pinch fruit off the cart. Tammy turned and shouted

–Get awa' o' that wi' ye, you McGraws!
and chased them round the cart and when he did that there were two more McGraws at the other side pinching apples and stuffing them up their jerseys. Then he turned and ran at them and the others did the same at the other side. Then they ran away up our close and he couldn't chase them and leave the cart or it might have been stripped by the time he got back.

Robert Cook and Alec Taylor were playing at bools in the gutter but seeing the apples and oranges made me hungry so I went up to the house. John was trying to put on a collar and tie and I asked him where he was going. He said he was going to the first house of the La Scala to see the Houston Sisters on the stage. I asked him who with and he said Lawrence McEvoy was coming for him.

–Where's my mammy?

–Up Glasgow Street for messages.

–Where's m'daddy?

–In the wee bed.

–Where's Annie?

–Out playing . . . Ask no questions and you'll be told no lies.

–Gi'es a piece and jam John, I'm hungry.

–Have you any more orders and have you any more questions?

–Go'on gi'es a piece John.

He went to the wee press and took out a loaf and put it on the breadboard and cut off a slice and put jam on it and it was rhubarb and ginger the best of all. I went to the window and John lifted me up on the chair and opened the bottom window and I leaned on the sill eating my piece and watching the chooky hens and the wagons shunting and the waves splashing over the Bath Rocks. I thought to myself I've been over there and I was standing on that bit that you can see sticking up and I did a stiff yin and I wondered if the Herald Street Gang would see it.

Then I heard m'daddy getting up out of the wee set-in bed and starting to get washed and changed to go out.

He put the kettle on to have a shave. Then there was a great shout from the street and the sound of feet running and echoing through the close.

–Hu-ll-aw!
Hu-ll-aw!

The Herald Street Gang all came running through the back-yard and started climbing over our wall, one after the other into the Fenian Row. As they ran across the yard, Big Alec Ballantyne took the feet from Jimmy Dodds running in front of him and Jimmy got up and ran to the wall and caught Ballantyne's leg as he tried to get over and pulled him back down again and they started to fight and punch each other. They fell up against one of the buckets and knocked it over, all the cabbage stalks and ashes falling out and they were rolling among all the rubbish and spreading it all over the yard.

–Get away out o' that wi' ye, ye bloody buggers
o' hell, I'll come down to ye and blatter yis!
Go on now, get ye's away out o' this, ye fiends
o' hell! Bejasus if I come down to ye!

Micky Boyle was shouting out of his window at them. They both got up, picking bits of cabbage off themselves and stopped fighting and shouted up at the window

–Away, ya blin' aul bastard!

Then there was a splash as Micky Boyle threw water out of his window at them and they jumped up on the wall and sat on the top and put their fingers to their noses up at the window and shouted

–Away back on the Irish boat where ye came from!

There was another splash.

–If I catch ye coming through here again I'll kick your arses for ye!

They jumped down the other side and ran through Do'e-Do'e Donaldson's close, still with their fingers to their noses.

Mammy came in with the messages from Glasgow Street and I turned and jumped down on the floor.

–Don't jump so hard on the floor Patrick. Bejings you'll be going through the roof to Missus Brannif's!

–Can I empty your bag, mammy?

–Yes, but watch them eggs!

I began to take the messages out of the bag and put them up on the table. The blue bag of sugar. Lipton's Tea. Danish Butter with golden buttercups painted on the paper. Lentils. A tin of peaches for Sunday. Creamola. Porridge Oats. A.1. Soap Powders.

–. . . Mary Cook's man, Bobby . . . from sea . . . Aye . . . An' he's stoatin' drunk . . . rollin' down the street . . . those bad women . . .

–Mammy, is Robert Cook's daddy a sailor? . . . Mammy . . . . Mammy . . . Is Robert Cook's daddy a sailor? Mammy, is he back from sea?

–Stop pulling at my skirt!

–Mammy!

–Would you not bother me. What is it?

–Is Robert Cook's daddy home from sea?

–Aye, that's right son . . . Aye . . Now stop pulling at my skirt.

–Mammy, can I go down the street a minute?

–Your tea'll be ready in a minute.

–Just for a minute, mammy.

–All right, away ye go. You be back up in five minutes for your tea.

I turned to run out the door.

–. . . Cook is standing in the Pen . . . The disgrace . . . she's ashamed . . . go out . . . aye he's stoatin' . . . a long time . . .

I ran down the stairs and into the street. I looked up and you could see heads sticking out of windows all the way down to Nicol's Bar where there was a crowd of people and a rammy going on. The women were all standing at the doors in their shawls looking up the street. George Hall came out on to the pavement opposite with a teapot and emptied it down the drain in the street.

–Hullo George!

–What do you want?

–I don't want nothing.
He went back in. He looked as if he had been crying. Josie Cook came round the corner from Bute Place.
–Hullo Josie!
–Hullo!
–Is your daddy home off the tanker?
–Cripes, yes!
He started running up the street. I ran along with him but when we got to the Big Pen his mother who was standing inside with Granny McNamee shouted out to Josie to come back but he ran on harder and I let him go in front. I dandered up the street after him.

The white apron of Mister Hughes the publican stood out in the crowd outside the pub and when I got nearer I could see sailors around, some square-rigged and some wearing rubber thigh boots and woollen tammies and light blue shirts that looked as if they had just been washed and some had red throat rags and some were covered in coal dust and some had daggers in their belts at the hip and all their faces were tanned and they all had beery bottles sticking out of their pockets. There were two big women all powdered and painted and bulging out of their tight dresses and wearing Russian boots and they had spiky eyelashes like the women in the pictures and their blouses were half open and when they bent over their diddies nearly came out. One of the weans shouted
–That's Black Maggie!
–Who?
–The big one with the black curly hair!
Josie was trying to get into the middle of this crowd and he was shouting
–Daddy, daddy! Come on! Daddy, my mammy's waiting for you!
Nobody was taking any notice of him.
–Daddy, you've got my mammy crying!
The man at the centre was wearing a blue jersey with crossed flags like Sailor McFarlane's and knee boots and a bunnet that looked as if it should have had a peak but it

didn't and he was trying to keep hold of a big golden cage with a parrot in it. All the lot of them kept falling about and kind of pulling each other and leaning against each other and the parrot was squawking away blue murder. I said to Josie

–Is that your faither?

–Aye.

–Is he a sailor?

–Aye, he's a bo'sun.

–What's a bo'sun?

–It's a kind of chief.

His father was laughing away all the time and standing right on the edge of the pavement trying to balance on one leg then he staggered on to the street and the other sailors and the big women were holding him up on both sides and he started to cross the street towards the seats where the old men were sitting.

–Raberd Jahn Cook!

He stopped dead halfway across the street.

–Raberd Jahn Cook!

We all looked down towards the Big Pen and Granny McNamee was standing in the middle of the street with her hands on her hips, shouting. Bobby Cook turned and said something to the other sailors and they slapped him on the back and then linked arms with the women and they all went away round Nicol's corner towards the harbour, waving back to Bobby as they went. Two of them stopped to give halfpennies to some of the weans that were following them. Mister Cook started to walk down the street and he was staggering from the wall to the edge of the pavement and back to the wall again and Josie ran over to hold his hand and we all followed along behind them. As they moved down the street the heads went in the windows but when they passed a window the heads came out again and the women were duking out and in their doors. Bobby stopped to speak to one of the women standing in her shawl and you could hear her all over the street giggling and laughing then he put his hand in his pocket and gave her wean some money and carried on down the street and the parrot was squawking all the time.

Granny NcNamee had gone through the Big Pen again and Bobby went into his house then Mary Cook ran in after him and closed the door. We stood around the door and you could hear a lot of loud voices inside. Then most of the heads began to go in the windows and we were all standing around Josie Cook's listening to the voices when Granny McNamee sprang out of the Pen and chased us all away. I went back up to the house and I met Annie going through the close.

As we went up the stairs we could hear the McGraws fighting and the door was banging as if somebody was being thrown against it and they were screeching and thumping then suddenly the door burst open and Peggy, Tommy and Wullie came running out screaming, followed by Missus McGraw and they half fell down the stairs to get away and they were all crying and Missus McGraw shook her fist at them and shouted down the stairs.

–Don't come back in ye bastards o' hell!

And all this time wee Geordie was sitting outside the door on the attic landing, doing number two and we had to hold our noses as we went past. My mammy said

–Come on you's, your tea is getting cold,

and we had fried slice.

After tea there came a shout up the stairs from Boyle's landing and John said that was Lawrence, he was away to the La Scala and he put his bunnet on, he always pulls the skip down over one eye. M'mammy said

–Don't be hooking your skip down like that, boy!

M'daddy said

–It makes you look like a gangster. Look at the oul' hooker down! The oul' hooker down. Are you going to hold up the cashier?

John's face got red and he said

–You's are always making a fool of me, so you are. I can wear my bunnet any way I like!

My daddy said

–You'll never get an oul' gerl with your cap like that! You'd better go and get us a pail of water before you go.

–I've always got to go and get a pail of water!

–Ah, go on, son, sure it won't take you a minute . . . do it for your mammy.

John went for the white pail.

–You may as well empty the black pail at the same time as you're going down. . . . Watch you don't frighten the weans in the backyard with that oul' hooker down cap!

He went out the door with the two pails, saying something under his breath.

I finished eating and looked for the cat. I couldn't see him and I asked my mammy where Toby was. She looked at my daddy and he looked at her and he said

–Better tell him. Go on, tell him.

M'mammy didn't say anything. I said

–What are you going to tell me, mammy, what are you going to tell me?

I felt the leadie taste in my mouth again and my stomach gave a kind of wee jump. She didn't say anything but gave a big sigh. Daddy said

–Toby's dead, son, we had to take him away and bury him.

I felt tears beginning to come up and I said

–Where did you bury him?

–In the sea.

–In the sea?

–Yes, he was sick and he died. . . . I think he just pined away. . . . John took him away in a bag and buried him in the sea.

Then the tears came right up into my eyes and began to run down my cheeks.

–Poor wee Toby!

Then Annie began to girn as well and mammy took us over to the fire by her side and told us to never mind and began to stroke our hair. She said Toby wanted to be with Mary, so he went away after her.

–Will Toby be in heaven, mammy!

–I'm sure he will.

–Did it have a white box as well?
–Yes.
–What kind of a box?
–A shoe box that your father's new boots came in.

My daddy was all dressed up for Saturday and he said he'd have to away out. Mammy said

–Don't be going in to that oul' Railway Bar.
–I might just go in for a couple of wee dumps.
–Go you to the pictures, there's a good picture on, Janet Gaynor is in it.
–What's it called?
–*The Seventh Heaven.*
–I'll just call in for a couple of wee dumps on the way.

Annie and me were still wingeing a bit and he came over and said

–If you die with a face like that, no-one will bury you.

We winged some more and he said to wait a minute and put his hand in his pocket and gave us a halfpenny each and we stopped girning. He said

–You'll have me stony broke so you will, you'll have me stony broke!

John came in with the two pails, put them down and said he was away and was out the door like lightning, and daddy said he was away after him, and he was out the door as well. Mammy shouted after him to watch himself and he shouted back he'd be all right.

I looked into the fire at mammy's knee and I thought I could see a hill between two coals and Mary and Toby were walking along together.

–Poor wee Toby.
–Never mind, my wee son, sure he'll be in heaven with Mary.
–Is heaven a good place?
–The best place of all.
–As good as the Princes Picture House?
–Better than anything.
–Can I go to heaven?
–If you're a good wee boy.

We sat up for a while looking at pictures in a book then it got darker and we went over to the window to see the lights coming on. Do'e-Do'e Donaldson's window lit up and you could see his mother going to the mantelpiece, then the blind came down and you could only see shadows. The lamp in Morgans' backyard came on only a wee bit. Then lamps began to come on along the Saltcoats promenade. Then a light from Ayr winked, and another and another until there was a string of them. The lights of Troon were more of an orange colour when they came on. And there was one light all by itself along at the end of the land—the heads of Ayr, John had told me—but they didn't look like heads to me, they weren't the shape of heads. Then the lighthouse on Paddy's Milestone began to flash out and in with its ray going through the sky. Then we watched some lights with our eyes glued to them to see if they were moving and if they were we knew they were boats. Mammy said

–I'd better light the lamp now, childher.

She took the lamp down off the mantelpiece and took the globe off and lit it and the flame shot up and was all sparking but when she put the globe on it changed and became smooth. Then she said it was time for bed and we had to strip off and be washed all over in a big tin bath in front of the fire. Then I put on my sleeping suit and Annie her nightdress and we went to bed, me at the bottom and Annie at the top.

I lay for a while watching my mammy sewing in front of the fire, then I moved my foot till I felt Annie's foot and I put my toes under her sole and moved them up and down and she burst out giggling and she couldn't stop and the more she giggled, the more I did it.

–Annie, be quiet now! Stop your giggling and go to sleep!

–It's Patrick, he's tickling me!

–Patrick, stop that!

So I stopped and I watched my mother again, sewing and patching in the lamplight till I dropped off to sleep.

I had a dream. In my dream my eyes came open halfway and I saw the attic in a dim dim light. Someone was falling about on the stairs and my mammy was crying and looking towards the stairs with her face all in creases and her hand over her mouth. She looked frightened and the firelight was flickering in her eyes. The door was thrown open and it smashed against the bed and John came in half-carrying and half-dragging daddy. His head was lying on his chest and his cap was falling off. Mammy came over and put her hand on his shoulder and he began to shout and throw his fists about. He caught mammy and gave her a shove and she fell over and nearly hit her head on the fender. Then he fell on the floor on his back and he was roaring and shouting. He got up on his feet and John went towards him to catch him but he drew his fist and punched John in the face and blood began to run out of his nose. Then he went after mammy with his fist flying and she screeched

–Jesus, Mary and Joseph, he'll kill me!

and ran down to the window. John came after him and got up behind him and caught him around the waist and dragged him away. And as he was being pulled away he got hold of the wee press and knocked it over and all the pots and pans fell out on the floor. Then my mother began to moan

–Sacred heart of Jesus help me! Look down on us this night! Ah, Dan, Dan, sure you're not in your right senses!

Dan dear, listen to me!

John was rastling with him and he managed to get him on to the chair that we won at the pictures. Then he loosened his tie and collar and took his boots off and every time he tried to get up, John forced him down again. John has got a big chest and he is very strong. M'mammy was hiding behind the dresser over by the window and she was crying and sobbing. Then daddy got quieter and quieter and he began to snore with his mouth open and John lifted him up all by himself and staggered with him over to the set-in bed and put him in and my mammy put her hand up to her lips and tiptoed over to the lamp and put it out and my dream faded with it.

12

I had a great feeling on Sunday morning while I was looking out of the window at the sea and the Bath Rocks all lonely and deserted and I smelt the Ayrshire bacon frying behind me. Everybody was clean and dressed in their best clothes and my good boots were polished and it was the same feeling that you get when it's a holiday or an uncle comes to see you. Mammy was to take Annie and me to the Children's Mass at ten o'clock but daddy was not up yet and he would go to the half-past-eleven with John.

He was just getting up as we left. He was groaning a bit and I saw him get down to the floor in his long white drawers as we went out the door. We haven't got a chapel and we have to get a motor to Saltcoats every Sunday or Holiday of Obligation, sometimes we can walk if the weather is good. We went to the Town Hall to catch the new motor that's started, Jimmy Stewart's. It's a brown one with canvas flaps and there is a special one on Sunday for the Children's Mass.

The motor stopped at the chapel, Our Lady Star of the Sea. She sometimes changes into a big blue star and shines away out behind Arran where the sea is deep. But she can only do that at week-ends because through the week she is the Help of Christians or the Mother of Mercy or the Mystical Rose. During the mass, m'mammy wouldn't let me crawl under the seats to the pipes to see if anybody would have dropped an odd halfpenny behind them. She made me sit doing nothing on the hard seat. The mass seemed to last forever. There was mumbling and moaning and mammy bowed her head and looked the same as when Mary went off in her white box. There was a long silence that seemed to go on for all eternity. You couldn't hear a pin drop so you couldn't. Then a wee bell rang. It sounded like a plunker inside a beery bottle. When I looked round everybody had their heads bowed down and some of them had beads hanging from their hands and all their faces looked like m'daddy's on Saturday when he puts his glasses on to study the form of the horses.

The bell rang three times and then there was a great big sigh of relief and everybody began to cough and clear their throats and move their feet and blow their noses and the boy beside me began to smell.

I thought I would never get out from the building and I began to imagine that maybe we were all being kept prisoners here forever and we would have to stay here until we starved. M'mammy kept whispering to me to stop fidgeting but I couldn't just sit there doing nothing. I held my nose with my fingers because of the boy next to me and turned to look at the woman kneeling behind me. Her eyes were watery and when she saw me she looked as if she had suddenly swallowed something the wrong way. I turned to look at the top of a tree blowing in the wind outside a window. It was a funny window with panes of glass all in the shape of wee diamonds. At the top, two of them were half broken and you could see the sky through the hole. There was a rope hanging down for opening the top bit and I wished I had got to the end of the seat nearest the wall so that I could play with it. Up at the top of the window near the ceiling there were cobwebs and some flies buzzing about then landing on the glass. Sometimes a bird would fly on to a branch of the tree.

I began to feel sorry because I could hear a motor passing by outside, fading away into the distance down the Ardrossan Road and then I thought I heard a clock ticking somewhere and someone sniffed and I was thinking yes we were here forever would I start to girn so that somebody would hear me and help me to escape.

Then all at once everybody jumped to their feet with a clatter and began to cough and blow their noses and then they all began to sing

–Hail Queen of Heaven,
The Ocean Star!

I didn't know she was the queen as well, I suppose that's why she has a crown sometimes.

–Guide of the wanderer,
Here below!

There were some people who were wanderers—John told me a story about one who wandered over the desert and found a gold mine—and she is the one who guides them with her torch when they get lost in the dark.

–Save us from Pearl!

That's the wee man who comes on Saturday with elastics on his book. I didn't know he was a bad yin.

–And from woe!

That's what Peter Milne shouts to his horse—Woe!—when it wanders away down the street when he is in for a drink.

–Star of the Sea!

Everybody shouted this bit louder, you could hardly hear your ears. She must be shining now away out behind Arran, I thought, I will look for it tonight before I go to bed.

–Pray for me!

Then there was a crush to get out.

M'mammy said it wasn't a bad day, she was going on with Sarah Brannif, we two could walk home along the shore if we liked and she would be getting the dinner so we were not to be too long. Annie said to come on and we walked away down the Ardrossan Road. All the houses along there have palings and a gate and a garden behind and a path up to the doors with glass panels in them and big brass door bells. Doctor McCann lives there and Murray the Fishmonger and Miss Reilly the school teacher. I went along pulling off the leaves sticking out through the palings. Annie looked a bit sick with ferntickles on her face and she had red hair too, but not golden like Mary's was, sort of ruddy. M'daddy always says to her

–Ginger, you're balmy!

She said I was to stop pulling the leaves off or I'd get her into a row and I said no I wouldn't. She said I would. I said no I wouldn't and she was to shut her gub. She said she would tell m'mammy. So I told her if she didn't shut up I'd hit her a kick with my boots and break her leg into three halves.

–You'd better not.

–I will sot!

–How'll you get home? There'll be nobody to take you home.

–Well, shut it then!

–Look, Patrick, there's the Iron Bridge.

Over the other side of the road there was a bridge made of iron strips with wooden steps up one side and down the other for people to cross over the railway. Then we came to a house called THE STUDIO beside the Parish Offices where m'daddy says the destichukes and the bootless bairns go. It's got funny windows. Then there was a prodesunt church with people outside holding big black books under their arms.

–Run past here, quick, Patrick, them are prodesunts!

She caught my hand and we ran till we came to the Galloway Burn where it comes out of the Plantation Woods. It runs under Ardrossan Road and comes out into a grass patch then under the promenade out on to the shore and into the sea. The water was gurgling and running over big stones that you could see at the bottom. I picked up some wee stones from the gutter and put my head through the pailings and began plopping them into the burn. White bubbles came from the shadows and I tried to bomb them as they went past. After a while Annie said to come on, and I said all right because I was feeling a bit hungry anyway.

The wind began to blow in our faces across the park in front of the promenade as we came out of Ardrossan Road. Annie said to look there was m'daddy, and I looked along the promenade, and there he was marching along like a soldier on parade on his way to half-past-eleven mass. The coat tails of his raincoat were flying in the wind, his cap was set squarely on the top of his head, he took great big giant strides with his feet flying out to the side, his moustache was twirled into points nearly down to his chin and his pipe was puffing away like billy-o.

We stopped and began to wave our arms at him, and then he saw us and waved back, but he didn't stop marching along. John was not with him so he must have been going with a pal. I got on my horse and I went away after him, galloping across the grass, Annie shouting where was I going, the wind blowing hard against me like in a storm. I had to go hard to catch him so I began whipping my horse on both sides with the loose reins and calling to come on, Silver King. I had to catch up with him before we got to the bad lands. I managed to get up to him at last and I drew alongside and threw myself off without stopping and caught hold of his hand.

–Have you any odd halfpennies, daddy?

He went marching along with me running alongside him to keep up.

–You'll have me stony-broke, so you will; you'll have me stony-broke!

–Ah, go'on, see if you've got an odd halfpenny, daddy, see if there's one at the bottom of the lining.

–Well, if there is, it's more than I know about!

I got to thinking about a stick of allycreesh and big caramels, and my teeth were watering.

–Bejings, you're right, would you not believe that, here's an ould mouldy halfpenny inside the lining of my waistcoat. It's been there so long, it's got blue mouldy. . . . What do you say, eh, squareshoulders?

We saw a picture called SQUARESHOULDERS about a boy who was called that played by Frankie Darro, and m'daddy sometimes calls me that for fun.

–Thank . . . you . . . Ta-ta. . . .

I jumped on the saddle and galloped away back over the prairie again, the grass was rushing past me and the clover and I was going even faster because the wind was behind me, and I spotted Annie away near the road and I had to get to her to warn her that Indians were going to spring on her from the Plantation Woods. I got to her just in time to save her getting scalpted. Looking back I saw my daddy just crossing the Galloway Burn, his legs going like scissors.

–I got a halfpenny.
–You didn't!
–I did.
–You didn't!
–I did.
–Let me see it.
–Naw!
–Keep it then!

Then I said if we went over to the sandy shore I'd show it to her, but she said no, I hadn't got one.

–I have! Come on!
–Well you must show it to me as soon as we go down the brae.
–All right.

We went away walking over the grass and the clover and the wee white flowers and the yellow pee-the-beds. Annie wanted to pick some up and I said if you pick them yellow ones they would make you pee the bed. She put her hand up to her mouth and went

–Oh! You swore!

I asked her what she was saying and she told me I was not to say that word. I told her she pee'd the bed anyway.

–I'll tell my mammy when we get home!
–You're always telling! I won't show you my mouldy halfpenny if you tell her, will you tell her?

She said well I wasn't to say it again or I'd go to the bad fire but I couldn't see any of the Herald Street Gang anywhere so I wasn't afraid of getting burned.

We got down the brae to the sandy shore and I took out my halfpenny and she looked at it and said she knew how to make it look like a new one.

–You do not.
–I do sot!
–You're telling a fib.
–I am not!
–You are sot! How can you do that?
–Give it to me and I'll show you.
–No, you'll keep it.

–No, I won't.

–Cross your heart and spit.

–All right, but I'm not going to spit!

So I said it was all right, seeing that she was a lassie and I gave it to her.

She knelt down on the fine sand, the kind that runs through your fingers, and I crouched beside her. She said

–You've to go down over the seaweed and get some wet sand . . . This is our house and I'll keep the door locked till you come back.

She made a ring with a wee bit of stick and sat down.

–Right,

I said. And I put some more harness on Silver King and backed him into the shafts of a cart painted green and red and led him by the reins down to the line of seaweed.

–Get up oul' horsy, go for gran!

I held him steady as he pulled the cart over the seaweed. We came to wee wormy rings and all those ridges with sea water in between that are the same shape as wood when you look up close to it. I stopped and put my head sideways and half-shut my eyes and it was just like looking close at the planks of wood that are under the straw mattress of the set-in bed.

–Woe!

Back!

Silver King is a great horse and he doesn't wander away like Peter Milne's horse. He stood quietly while I loaded the cart up with wet sand then I turned him round and led him back up to the gate of the house again.

–Here's your wet sand, missus.

–Right. Bring it in and put it in the coalhouse.

Then she took the mouldy halfpenny and put it in the wet sand in her hand and began rubbing it with her fingers.

–I'll just let my horse out of the cart.

–What did you say?

I let Silver King out of the shafts and took some of his harness off. I left the cart in the stable and let the horse wander down to eat some seaweed. I only had to whistle for him and he would come running. I went back over and stood outside the house.

–Have you got a garden?

–Eh?

–Have you got a garden in your house?

–Yes.

–Can I come through the gate?

–Yes, it's open.

I walked through the gate and went up the path into the house and sat down on the big chair and watched Annie rubbing the halfpenny. It began to shine through the sand as it dribbled away through her fingers. She asked for more wet sand and I put some in her hand and the halfpenny was shining more and more until at last it looked like a big silver shilling. She gave it to me and I said that was great, it was a magic trick, was she a magician? She said

–No, I'm the Fairy Queen.

The clock of the English Church began to strike and we looked away up the front of it, right up to the spire. On top of the spire is a sailing ship painted gold with four iron rods sticking out saying N,S,E,W. I looked at the ship and it looked as if it was moving. It was sailing through the clouds and not heaving and I could see the sails full out and the rigging and the cabins and the flag at the stern. I said to Annie

–Is that as big as the ships in the harbour?

–Yes, it's bigger, it's a monster.

–How did they get it up there?

–They must have pulled it up with a crane.

–Has it got a crew on it?

–Yes.

–How do they get their dinner?

–They must climb down the spire.

–It's sailing!

–No, it isn't.

–Yes, it is. It's sailing through the clouds.

I stared a long time at it sailing through the sky, trying to see if I could see any sailors, and I thought I saw one moving on the rigging, then Annie asked me if I was going to spend my halfpenny. I said yes, we'd go to Missus Brekenridge's and get some broken toffee and she could have some for making the halfpenny shine. So we went back through the fine sand, our feet sinking into it like the desert, and up the brae, over the grass, past the green iron closets that smell like m'mammy's ammonia, across the street, past the church, through the Station Gates, along to Mary Barbour's corner into Hill Street then Hill Place to Missus Brekenridge's wee shop. Some of the Hill Street Gang were in the street and they were marching around in a ring singing

–Coperative, Coperative,
Give me no more of your cheese!
The last cheese I got,
It stuck in my throt,
And gave me Appentis Disease!

They didn't take any notice of us and we got the toffee and went back across Princes Street and sat up on the window of the Union Bank of Scotland eating it. We were looking at the palings running along the railway beside the Station Gates. Above them were billboards and on them was another sandy shore and words. There was a woman with a great big striped balloon and she had a moustache. There was a picture of the Arran Boat but it wasn't the Atlanta or the Glen Sannox or the Juno. There were pictures of the Belfast Boat and the Isle of Man Boat and that one looked like the King Orry. Then a big long sandy shore with a pier sticking out with millions of people on it and it was all colours of the rainbow and underneath, three words were stuck together, DUN and KER and QUE.

Where the palings run down to the Commercial Hotel and make a wee corner, the wind was blowing some bits of coloured paper around in circles. We got down off the window and went over to see what we could find. I got a motor ticket. There were some coloured paper streamers and an apple core and confetti and a bit of newspaper and a matchbox and a torn paper Woodbine poke the same as John sometimes gets. I was tying the streamers around the palings when

Annie said to come on, we'd have to go for our dinner. I said to wait a minute. I wanted to pick up the bits of confetti one by one, load them on the cart and drop them through the palings on to the railway line where all the wires and wee wheels are. I did this and I was looking through the railings where you can sometimes see the rails changing. Annie said to come on or we'd get into a row. I said to wait a minute and went back to get more confetti. I loaded it on the cart, dumped it and went back for more.

–Come on, Patrick!

–Wait a minute.

–Well, I'm away without you!

I opened my mouth and roared at the top of my voice and she didn't move. I went and got some more confetti.

–I'm going if you don't come!

I roared again and shouted that I'd tell my daddy, and she didn't move. Her mouth went sort of down at the corners.

–Come on, Patrick, or you'll get me into a row, look at your hands, you're covered in muck and it's all over your trousers.

I was feeling a bit hungry anyway so I said

–All right. But I'm not coming with you!

I walked a good bit behind her and she kept looking back, and when we got into Harbour Place the voices of the Hill Street Gang had come over the roofs as they always do to the boys and lassies playing in the street and now they began to sing as well.

–Coperative, Coperative,
Give me no more of your cheese!
The last cheese I got,
It stuck in my throt,
And gave me Appentis Disease!

We went up for our dinner and it was barley soup with lumps of mutton in it and some tatties. And after that we had some peaches out of a tin because it was Sunday and m'mammy let me drink what was left of the juice out of the tin.

13

After our dinner, m'daddy went over to the fire and sat on the leatherette chair and m'mammy sat on the other one. In a while, John went out for a walk and Annie got ready to go to Sunday School. M'mammy said

–Come on, Patrick, you should be going too, you'd better go with Annie.

–I don't want to go.

–Oh, but you'll have to.

–I'm not going.

I went over to my daddy and climbed on his knee. I looked at his eyes and they were black and so were his eyebrows and they went up in the middle like the Iron Bridge and his hair was black as well but his moustache was a bit gingery.

–I don't want to go to Sunday School, daddy.

–What d'you say, my wee son?

–I don't want to go to Sunday School, daddy, I'm not going.

He said to m'mammy

–Ah, sure he's time enough going to Sunday School, let the wee fella stay at home.

My mammy went

–Tit! Tit! Tit!

So Annie went out to go with Margit Morgan and Mary McFarlane to Sunday School and I stayed at home. I went up to the table and there was a knife lying on it. I turned it so that the edge was sticking up and it was an Ice-Cutter, the Nascopie, the boat that Wullie Brannif was away on and Big Eddie McGinn, the Bo'sun. John says it sails to the frozen north, to somewhere called Hudson's Bay and when it cuts all the ice up there it comes back with a polar bear in a cage on the deck and penguin birds. I put my finger to the stern of the knife for a rudder and began to steer it through the docks and through all the channels. You must keep your finger right at the stern and you can't move the ship from the side or pull it from the bow for that would be cheating. I was sailing from Ardrossan to Hudson's Bay and I was steering the ship slowly past the sugarbowl lighthouse and then trying to swing it round to miss an iceberg but without moving my finger from the stern. I was the captain and I was out on the bridge. M'daddy and mammy were talking at the fire.

– . . . think he's from Belfast as well . . . you remember him well . . . Who's this now?

–Ah, sure yis . . . many's the time I seen him walking down the Oldpark Road . . .

– . . . the Cave Hill . . . married one of the McBrides . . .
Sure, look at the jobs you had . . . And you never stayed in one of them . . .

– . . . aye, the great oul jobs . . . McCaw, Stevenson and Orr . . . used to say to me . . . And how is Daniel this morning? I want you to polish the brass plate . . . They had a lovely brass plate outside, ye know . . .

–Brass plates? . . . Aye, I know they did . . . had the chances. . . .

I got past the iceberg with only an inch to spare and I was sailing for between the breakwater and Winton Pier.

– . . . Post Office was the best job you ever had . . . you in the Post Office as well . . .

–Mister O'Neill speaking for me as well . . .

–Your Uncle John . . . flung it all in their faces . . . the disgrace . . .

–Aye . . . disgrace . . .

–And your poor oul' mother, God rest her soul . . . never forget the day . . .

–It was the drink you see . . .

–Rolling in the gutter . . .

–Sure, I know . . . never have sense . . .

–In your uniform, too . . .

–the telegrams still in my pouch.

I could just miss the breakwater if I swung around hard to the lighthouse.

–Now, I'm only an oul' labourer . . .

– . . . we should have stayed in Belfast . . .

–wouldn't say . . . never a bit . . . Aye, no nor yis . . . He wouldn't say aye, no nor yis . . .

–Soda farls . . . then big Barney Hughes's baps . . . like old Belfast . . . at the Donegal Quay . . . drivin' out to . . .

– . . . your Uncle John . . . the quare oul' tear . . . quare times . . . there's no work, sure . . .

–I know . . . otherwise I wouldn't be here . . .

–pity you couldn't get an oul' job . . .

–Bejings if I could, Dan wouldn't be here . . . Dan would be walking down the Oldpark Road this night . . .

I stopped engines after I had missed the breakwater and sailed past the pier. I gave the order to drop the anchor. Then I went over to m'daddy.

–Daddy, is there a harbour in Belfast?

–What's that, wee fella, a harbour? Aye, there is that.

–Have they got big boats?

–Aye they have that. Have you never heard of oul' Harland and Wolff's shipyard where they build the Ocean Liners . . .

–Do you come from Belfast, daddy?

–Aye, and your mammy as well.

–Do you, mammy?

–Yis, that's right son.

She looked at m'daddy's eyes and he looked at her eyes.

–That wee fella hears every word you say.

–Aye, it all goes in here ye know.

Daddy put his finger to the side of his head and turned it like a screw. He said

–Is that an oul' boat you have there?

–Yes, it's the Nascopie.

–I thought I recognised the cut of it . . . Well, you'd better go and take it in to harbour, otherwise it'll sink.

–I've got the anchor down.
–Well let me see you pull it up then.
–Will you look at me doing it?
–Yis.

I went over and I began to haul up the anchor again and come back across the sea to Ardrossan again because all the ice had been cut.

–I think you're going to be an' oul sailor like your Gran-daddy.
–Was he a sailor, daddy?
–He was a captain.
–That's higher than a Bo'sun, isn't it daddy?
–Yes, he's the chief of the whole ship.
–What was the name of the ship, daddy?
–The Elvira. The S.S. Elvira.
–If I sailed out to sea would I be able to see Toby floating on the waves?
–Aye, ye might at that. Sure, maybe he's got a wee boat of his own.

M'mammy came to lift all the things off the table and, as all the ice was cut, I told the crew we were going to drydock and I went over to the window and looked out to the sea past the end of Arran and daddy and mammy's voices were murmuring away behind me and sometimes I could hear the voices in my head and sometimes the waves.

– . . . think that wee cat died of a broken heart . . .
–Aye, he pined away . . .
– . . . loved him, so she did
– . . . pined away . . . how it used to go up on the bed and lay down and cry
– . . . think she was a wee saint . . .
–she's in heaven.
–Oh, you can be sure . . . A great wee girl . . .
– . . . things off the street . . . yis, I caught her eating sweets that she'd picked up . . .
–them bloody oul' lozenges . . . scented sweeties . . . A lot of oul' rubbish . . . think that was how she got her death, so it was . . .

If I half-shut my eyes, maybe I could see a wee boat sailing over the waves with Toby standing up on the bridge. And maybe Mary would be sitting in the stern with her long red hair blowing out like a flag.

– . . . round the corner . . . d'ye remember? . . . We saw those Lascars off a ship . . . looked into my face . . . mammy she said, mammy . . . I doobt them's blacks . . .

I doobt them's blacks . . .

Yis, I doobt them's blacks she said, God rest her wee soul . . .

If ever I went to sea on a big boat I would look for Toby and Mary and I would rescue them in a lifeboat. Maybe Toby would be washed in at the rocks down the Inches sometime. Maybe Mary would meet the Star of the Sea when she was going through the sky in her white box.

– . . . one time . . . believe this . . . said, aye she said . . . Aye, she said, Annie don't you be asking my mammy for money because she's poor and canny give you any . . .

– . . . Go along wi' ye!

– . . . sure as I'm sitting here . . . was very wise, ye know . . .

– . . . like a wee wumman . . .

– . . . she was a wee saint right enough . . . That's right, she was too good for this world, so she was.

The Herald Street Gang were out chasing each other over the wash-house roofs. Big Alec Ballantyne was the gang leader and Jimmy Dodds, the next one. Some ran along the wee wall leading to Morgans' backyard and climbed on to our wash-house roof. The tin was clanging like a bell. Then they walked along a wall with broken glass bottles sticking out of it and they only had their bare feet. Then on to Do'e-Do'e Donaldson's roof, along the wall at the end of our backyard, up on to the wash-house roofs of the Big Pen and then Granny McNamee came out and shouted

–Get away to hell off that roof!

Paddy McNamee was chopping up the old driftwood outside

his coalhouse but he threw down his hatchet and came over beside Granny McNamee and began shouting along with her. But you couldn't hear what he was saying because of his beard. It just sounded like he was roaring. His swallow-tail coat was jumping up and down.

–Beardie! Aul' Beardie!
Aul' Cheat the barber!

They were all roaring and laughing and running round the roof.

–Paddy McNamee wi' a hole in his knee!
Irish Paddy!
Irish Paddy!

Paddy McNamee was shaking his fists and roaring through his beard and jumping up and down and Granny McNamee was shouting along with him. Then the gang all began to chant together. Some of the wee ones had their feet cut with walking on the glass and every time they put their foot down it made a bloodstain on the roof and some of them had their teapots hanging out and all of them had the shirt-tails sticking out of a big hole in their trousers and snotters were hanging from their noses and their faces were covered with muck and their hair sticking up on end. Some of them didn't have a shirt but wore their trousers with galluses over their bare shoulders. They all sang together

–Ir-ish Pa-ddy!
Ir-ish Pa-ddy!

Then Bobby Cook came running out in his sailor's jersey and was making to climb up on to the wall to get on to the roof and there was a scattering and scuffling in the gang to get away and they were fighting each other to get off and on to another wall and they all went running along the top, balancing as they ran, and got to Smith's wash-house roof and climbed down off that and ran through a close into the Fenian Row and you could hear their voices echoing in the close.

–Hullaw! Hullaw!

I asked m'mammy if I could go out and play in the close and she said

–Yes, away you go. Don't wake your daddy up.

He was snoring in the armchair. Out on the landing, Geordie McGraw was crouching down doing number two on the landing and Davy was standing beside him. Davy said

–What ye lookin' at? I'll give you a belt on the nose, Connor!

I said I would give him a belt on the ear and put my fists up. He took a punch at the air and I worked my fists up and down then he put his hand on Geordie's shoulder and I went down the stair and out the close. I could hear singing as I got to the end.

–My cup's full an' Granny Noper!

The hallelujahs were in the street, standing around in a ring outside the Church of the Nazarene. I went down and climbed up on the palings with the other boys to watch.

–May the Lord save me,
I'm as happy as can be,
My cup's full an' Granny Noper!

There was a wee man in a black suit playing what looked like a melodeon—a concertina, John told me—and it had a nice sad sound like the organ in the chapel.

–Granny Noper!
Granny Noper!
My cup's full an' Granny Noper!

Mister Slicer who lives on the other side of the Big Pen walked into the middle and began to shout and wave his arms about. We were playing at shoving each other off the wall.

– . . . Moses . . . say to thee . . . sin . . . down off the . . . Oh, my beloved friends. . . .

I was hanging on to the palings with one hand and punching Alan Clark in the stomach with the other. He was trying to get me off the wall.

–Brethren . . . Open your hearts . . . Love. . . .

We both fell on to the pavement and I caught him round the neck and was trying to force his head back.

– . . . Seek him . . . Come to him. . . .

We got up off the pavement and then all the boys and lassies chased each other in and out the hallelujahs around the ring.

– . . . The blood of the . . . The Love of the Nazarene. . . .

We were catching hold of the big women's skirts as we ran around and swinging on them. Some of them spun around.

– . . . Seek ye the kingdom . . . Love thy neighbour . . . Take my yoke upon thee. . . .

Suddenly Mister Slicer rushed at one of the boys and kicked him on the backside. We ran away out of range to a safe distance and started to shout at them.

–Hallelujah! Slice o' dumpling!
Hallelujah! Slice o' dumplin'!

Mister Slicer put his black book under his arm and went over to stand in the ring again.

– . . . Page one hundred and nineteen . . . Now brethren. . . .

They all began to sing

–At the cross!
At the cross!
Were you there, were you there?
At the cross!

They all lined up and marched away down the street led by Mister Slicer, all singing and the wee man playing his concertina. We all marched along behind them singing and shouting

–At the cross!
At the cross!
Where we played at pitch and toss,
And the polis came and chased us all away!
And we ran,
And we ran,
And we fell into a cornbeef can,
And now we're in jail for sixty days!

The procession marched down the street and all the women came to their windows and Sailor McFarlane took the pipe out of his mouth and laughed out loud. All the way down the street we sang

–Hallelujah! Slice o' dumplin'!
Hullaw!
Hullaw!
Aw, mah ma's big tumshie!

Wee Billy Munn,
Fell and skint his bum!
Wee Billy Munn,
Fell and skint his bum!

Hullaw! Hullaw!

At the cross!
At the cross!
Where we played at pitch and toss. . . .

14

After the hallelujahs marched round the corner away to the Town Cross, we all went in for our tea. We had some red cheese and then I went over to the window with John and he was telling me about Silver King and how I'd better hurry up and get big and it was getting dark and the sea wall along the Inches Road was disappearing. Mammy said

–John, son, you'd better go down and get a pail of water before it gets dark.

–Oh, all right. I suppose I'd better empty the black pail as well.

I said

–You're strong John, aren't you? Like Targa the Terrible! You could carry the two pails on your wee pinky, couldn't you?

–Of course I could. Am I not Targa!

I asked him to let me see his muscles and he rolled his shirt sleeves right up and bent his arm and his muscles stood up like footballs.

–Am I not Targa!

Then he asked me to hang on his arm and I hung on like on a swing and it felt just like an iron bar. He lifted it slowly up in the air and I went with it. Then m'mammy said

–Come on Tarzan, it's time you got that water up before it gets too dark.

M'daddy lit the lamp and poked the fire up. John let me down and picked up the white pail. When he bent for the black pail he said

–Oh, what a smell!

and went down the stairs.

At the window, I heard the spicket running down in the

backyard and the pails rattling then after a while we heard his voice crying

–Open—the door!

That's what we shout in a kind of song at the bottom of the wooden stairs when we come home in the dark so that someone will open the door and throw a light on the stairs.

Annie held the door open and the light of the lamp shone out on to the landing. It was quiet because most of the McGraws were still out chasing the hallelujahs. John came in and put the pails away and we all sat around the fire, Annie on one fender stool, me on the other, John on a wooden chair and mammy and daddy at both sides. The wind whistled through the keyhole and Annie said it couldn't get to us, we were cosy. M'daddy hissed out of the side of his mouth.

–Don't move . . .
Don't make a sound . . .

I felt my stomach jump and my back tingle and I saw Annie's face getting white and the corners of her mouth went down and she said

–Oh, mammy, daddy, what is it!

She looked as if her face was getting ready to cry then daddy hissed again

–Would you hould your whisht, gerl!
Don't make a sound . . .
Keep still . . .

I sat, not moving and looking at Annie and she was trying to keep her face from being frightened and the corners of her mouth were right down now.

–D'you see him?

–Oh, mammy, da—

–Whisht!

We all turned to stooky again. M'mammy was looking at daddy with the same look that she has when they argue about his pay on Friday night.

–Just look down beside the bottom corner of the wee set-in bed . . .
D'y'see the wee fella?

Whisht!
D'y'see him lookin' out?

There must be a wee man somewhere down on the floor walking about, a wee man about two inches high like you see in FAIRYLAND TALES. What was he doing in our attic? Maybe there was a pot of gold under the set-in bed.

–Look at him!
He's coming out . . .

Annie's ferntickles looked black against the white of her face and she was sick-looking again. I was glad that I was sitting beside John who could fight anybody, maybe even Wullie Brannif. I was afraid to look towards where m'daddy was signing.

–Look, a grey wee furry fella . . .
Whisht! Here he comes . . .

Some cheese crumbs were lying on the hearth where they had fallen after mammy had thrown the table clearings into the fire.

–Hold still, there he is now on the hearth!

I looked down and there was a wee mouse not the size of nothing running in and nibbling at the cheese crumbs.

–Look, he's just under Annie's feet . . .

Annie gave a squeal and leapt up and m'mammy shouted

–Jesus, Mary and Joseph!

The two of them ran and jumped up on the big bed and pulled their legs up underneath them and then John and daddy and me were laughing so hard we couldn't stop.

The wee mouse turned and disappeared like lightning under the set-in bed and after a while mammy and Annie started to laugh as well till we were all laughing together and the tears were running out of m'daddy's eyes and they had lines running out all round them like stars.

–Here, it might have climbed into one of me oul' pipes!

That made Annie worse and she was holding her stomach and she couldn't stop laughing.

–Be the hokey fly!

Daddy jumped up and dived under the bed and then he

came out with a pipe. He held it up, turned it upside down, shook it and said

–B' the hokey fly, if you don't come out of there, wee fella!

I had fallen across John's knee I was laughing so much and then daddy said

–No, it's all right, I can have an oul' smoke

and he took out his knife and snedded some tobacco in the palm of his hand.

–You can come down again, the wee fella's away back into his hole . . .

Annie and mammy came back down from the bed still laughing a bit and sat round the fire again and daddy said

–Ah, sure it wouldn't touch you . . . A mouse is all right you know . . . sure they're no harm at all. . . .

Mammy said

–I'm afeard they would run up your legs.

Annie gave a wee squeal and m'daddy said

–No, they wouldn't touch you . . . Mice are clean, so they are.

–Aye, they're clean. That's right enough.

–Now, a rat is a different thing . . . the rat is the devil . . . and he's dirty. . . .

–Oh, don't be talking about them rats, Dan . . . I saw enough of them . . . D'ye remember?

–Aye, I do that.

–That other oul' kip of a place we lived in. When this big rat came right up on the bed and nearly frightened the wean out of its wits!

–Aye, the poor wee soul.

– . . . I'm sure Dennis never got over that, you know . . . It's no wonder he died in convulsions.

–Aye, that's right . . . Ah, don't be talkin' about it now, you'll frighten the weans. . . .

Daddy had his pipe filled and he lit it and began to puff away. Every so often he would lean over to spit in the fire. If he missed the hot coals sometimes it would sizzle on the grating. After a while John was humming a song under his breath. M'mammy said to him

–What time do you have to go to the motor in the morning?

–Half-past-seven at the garage.

–Wasn't that good, your son getting that job with Jimmy Stewart, even if it's only a few shillings a week?

–Aye, that's great son, that's great. You're going to be a fine man and a great help to your mother.

John has got a job taking the money and giving out tickets on Jimmy Stewart's motor. He's to wear a leather bag and he's got to learn to wind up the engine and then when the motor is going he gives out the tickets and goes and stands outside the door on the step at the back holding on to the brass rails.

I asked John if he was going to make some smokeboard and m'mammy said to him that he was the smokeboard expert, to make some and give us all a wee drap. M'daddy said it should be good smokeboard because of the blowdown. When the wind turned every so often it blew the smoke back down the chimley and it all came pouring out from under the smokeboard and filled the attic. When it got too full of smoke we had to open a window wide and then it got freezing cold and sometimes it blew the lamp out.

John got out the frying pan that had the dripping still lying in it from breakfast time. Then he went to the pot with all the tatties in it from the dinner and emptied it into the pan. Then he put it on the fire and while they were frying he was champing them up with the wooden champer and sprinkling pepper and salt on them.

When they were ready we all got some in a wee plate or a saucer and we sat round, eating them with our fingers and licking them after. There were brown fried-up hard bits among them and they had a great smoky peppery taste.

After we were finished, John began to sing *Home in Pasadena* and m'mammy said them oul' modern songs were no good and m'daddy said then why wouldn't she give us her favourite?

We looked at her and she started to sing something about other lips and other eyes and it was a kind of old fashioned song that went up very high. Her eyes were half closed and m'daddy sat puffing at his pipe and looking into the fire with crinkly eyes and her voice went on up high sometimes like a bird singing, all the time the wind whistling along with her through the keyhole and then the smoke came pouring from under the smokeboard back into the house and it made our eyes smart and we all began to cough and m'mammy had to stop singing.

15

Her eyes looked at us over the black rims of her glasses.

–Who made you?

–God made me!

–Why did God make you?

–God made me to know him, love him, serve him in this world and be happy with him forever in the next!

We all had to bring a penny each for a catechism and we sat with the wee books in front of us while the teacher read out the questions and we sang out the answers together.

The next world is another world where you go after the Day of Judgement. I don't know what shape it is. There are three places in it, Heaven, the Bad Fire and Purgatory. You're not to say hell because that's a bad word and it's a sin and it makes your soul black, blacker than the night, blacker than coal and if you were to die after you said it you would go straight to the bad fire and the devil would stick his fork in you and toast you on the fire like my daddy toasts his kippers.

Your soul is a kind of space inside you between your neck and your stomach. It should be filled with grace which is like shiny cotton wool. But every time you commit a sin, a bit of it turns black and after a lot of sins it gets so black it looks like a bag of soot. Then you're not in a fit state to get in the gates of heaven and if you were to die like that without a priest getting there in time you would go straight to the devil quicker than a flash of lighting. If your soul is filled with grace you can get to heaven any time whenever you die.

Heaven is a kingdom in the next world. It has great big pearly gates where Saint Peter stands examining the souls as they come to him. Some of them try to duke past with black souls. But he spots them and sends them down to Satan. If heaven has got gates it must have a wall round it, something like the sea wall on the Inches Road but I don't know what it's made of. I asked the teacher what the wall was made of if the gates were made of pearl but she didn't answer me.

There are saints in heaven and angels and Mary the mother of God and Joseph and Saint Peter and all the ones who were at the Crucifixion. Both the men and women saints wear the same kind of clothes, sort of long robes but you can tell the men saints because they've all got beards. They move about heaven on clouds. Heaven is the greatest place there is, even greater than Fairyland or the Wild West or Belfast. The angels don't wear robes because they haven't got bodies except for one, the Angel Gabriel. All the rest of them have just got heads with no neck but two wings coming from under their chins. They all have fat round faces with red cheeks and curly hair and look like the photo of wee Dennis that died in convulsions. They just fly about among the clouds, going messages for the saints. Some of them land on a cloud and stay there for a while playing a harp. Sometimes they come down to earth when there is a new saint coming along. The Angel Gabriel's got a big book to read.

God sits on a throne in the middle of heaven surrounded by clouds and stars and all the ones who were at the Crucifixion. You can see his heart and there is a light all round it and a band of jaggy nettles. There is a light round his head as well and a big ring floating in the air above it. All the ones in heaven have these but none of them is as big as God's. Mary sits on a throne not far from God. She always wears blue clothes and He always wears red clothes no matter when. They don't have a cat or a dog but there is a lamb which carries a pole with a wee flag stuck on the end in one of its front paws. It just runs about heaven and I suppose they have some place to keep it at night. It doesn't need a saucer of milk or anything like that because nobody ever gets hungry in heaven. You go to Purgatory if your soul is half black and half white. While you are there, all your family and all your friends pray for you at home. If you can get some priest to pray for you as well, that's all the better but a mass said for you is best of all. Everybody should be storming heaven for you with their prayers and this makes your soul whiter and whiter and takes away the black stains. Then, when it is completely white you get into heaven.

After we had finished the catechism a priest came in and talked to us. He said we were to be good boys and girls and not to sin. Because every time we committed a sin it made Christ's wounds bleed again. It made me feel very sad and sorry for God who is the same as Christ to be suffering all the time and bleeding away. I know what it's like when I fall and skin my knee. Before he went we all stood up and sang

–Hail Saint Jo-
Seph spouse of Ma-
Ree guardian of
The sacred child

When the death
Shades roundus ga-
Ther teach oh tea-
Chus how to die!
Teach oh tea-
Chus how to die!

In the afternoon we had raffia work and cutting coloured paper into shapes and sticking them on white pages. Then it was home-time and I ran round to the gates to meet Annie. A lot of boys and lassies were all standing around in a crowd, shouting and talking and there was no sign of the matchbox anywhere. Then Annie told me that the matchbox had gone on fire and burned all away and that was the end of it and we wouldn't see it again.

So we all had to walk home from Saltcoats. Me and Annie, Lizzie Boyle, Margit Morgan, Robert Cook, Joseph Cook and James McAteer's wee brother, Eddie. We went down Manse Street, past the Saltcoats War Memorial, past the chapel, down the Ardrossan Road to the Galloway Burn and over the grass to the shore opposite the Ardrossan Academy. That's where the children of the big bugs go. They all live in the swanky houses up the North Shore and Parkhouse Road and Eglinton Road and places like that. They were just coming out to go home. You could see them a mile away in their red blazers with gold braid round the edges, a gold badge on the pocket and a school cap the same with the badge on the front and their stockings are never wrinkled.

We broke away from the lassies and went with some big boys, George Hall and John Smith and Big Josie McAteer who is nearly left school. They led us along a path at the other side of the road to the Academy and we all began to shout

–Academy mugs,
Squeeze the bugs,
Chew the cats,
And eat the rats!
Academy mugs!

They didn't shout anything back but went along in their straight stockings, carrying leather cases and not school bags like us.

–Academy mugs!

–Your faither wouldn't give you a job if you were starving!

They began to run.

–Who put the blind woman out on the cold stones!

–Who gave my mother short weight!

–Rotten eggs!

Then Big Josie and the other big boys shouted hullaw and we shouted it as well and charged with them across the road and chased the Academy mugs. We surrounded some of them in the gateway of a big house and the big boys began to punch the Academy boys who were the same size. We went for the wee ones the same size as us and I got one and punched him on the chin and knocked him into a flower bed. We kicked their cases about and some of them burst open. Then they ran away, some of them leaving their caps behind and we chased them all the way to the South Beach Road leading to the Plantation and as they ran up there we stopped and shouted after them

–Academy mugs,
Squeeze the bugs,
Chew the cats,
And eat the rats!

And the big boys shouted

–Your faither's a robber!

–We want bread!

–Academy mugs!

After they had retreated over the brae to their own territory where we couldn't follow, or else we would have got the same dose as we gave them, the big boys said they were going to run it home and they began to trot along together keeping step. We couldn't keep up with them so went back to the lassies who were walking along at the edge of the shore. Annie said we were not to be going with those big boys and fighting or she'd tell m'mammy. I told her if she didn't shut up I'd shove her in the water and drownd her. We went home.

In the evening m'daddy was smoking his pipe by the fire. M'mammy had a sad face and she kept going tit, tit, tit.

– . . . what we'll do . . . terrible . . . not a penny piece in the house . . . not a penny piece. . . . And it only Monday night . . . no living in this world at all. . . .

M'mammy turned to John and said

–John, son . . . I think you'll have to go out the road.

–I don't want to go, mammy. . . .

–There's not a copper in the house.

–Somebody'll see me going in. . . . Even in the street,

they know where you're going if they see you carrying a parcel.

–I don't know what we'll do. . . . You's all have to be fed. . . .

Daddy spat in the fire and said

–You know I'd give you more if I had it. . . . But sure I'm only an oul' common five-eight.

–I know you would, sure. . . . Have you not got a wee tanner in the bottom of your pocket?

–I haven't got a louse, as the man said. . . . No I haven't got a louse. . . . Maggie, sure, I only wish I had more to give you. . . . I only have an oul' labourer's wage. . . .

–That's the trouble with being honest. . . . We're too honest, so we are. . . . The McGraws never want. . . . They can go over the railway and pinch the coal out of the wagons . . . pinch the herrings from the boats coming in the harbour . . . lift the fruit from the carts . . . You get on better in this world if you're a heathen, so you do.

–Never mind, Maggie . . . John'll go out the road. . . . Have you not a pair of blankets he can take. Nobody'll know the difference. . . .

My mother got out a pair of blankets and daddy took them from her. He got John to take his pullover off and while m'mammy turned her back, he took down his trousers. Then m'daddy wrapped the two blankets around John's body, tied them with a big bit of string and pulled his trousers up over them. He didn't need to put his pullover on again or a jacket. He just had an old raincoat put on him, buttoned up to the neck and his cap on, pulled down over one eye as usual. M'mammy said

–Away you go now son, it will take you some time to walk out to Saltcoats. . . . Try to get seven shillings. . . . Ask for nine shillings and he'll give you seven.

John looked fat going out the door but when he came back he was the same size again. He said

–I could only get six shillings, mammy, he would only give me six shillings.

–He's an oul' robber so he is, son.

Daddy spat in the fire and said

–He wouldn't give you a lick of his cagh, so he wouldn't!

–Tit, tit, tit! Dan, don't forget yourself in front of the weans!

John said

–I duked in the door and nobody saw me. . . . But guess who was in? . . . Beanie McMullin down the street was in with a pair of her father's boots. . . . We didn't let on we saw each other.

–Six shillings, my wee son, well you did well for your mammy . . . Away you round to Coyle's and get a fish supper and two penny pokes of chips. . . . Have you got the ticket?

John gave her a ticket with very wee writing on the back and she put it in the jug where she keeps the rent money. Then he went to get the fish and chips and as he went out the door m'mammy said to get himself a tuppenny packet of Woodbines for being a good wee son and John's eyes lit up and his face got a bit redder and he smiled from one ear to the other.

16

– . . . Is it the same as when you strike a match, John?

–No, it's the men are striking.

–What are they striking?

I ran along beside him as he walked towards the Inches, carrying a big shovel with a long handle that he got the loan of from somebody down the street. I was carrying an old coal bag that we got from Peter Milne.

–It's because the big bugs won't pay them enough money for their work.

–Are they working?

–Some of them can't get a job. . . . Some of them can't get to work because there's no trains or motors. . . . That's why we can't get any coal.

–Is that why you're digging for duff?

–Yes.

We got down the rubbish dump, went across the Inches and began to climb the Bath Rocks. The tide was out as far as it could go and the Cruiben Rocks were both standing high and dry like islands.

–Why can we not get coal from the railway wagons over the wall like the McGraws?

–Because that's a sin and we would go to the bad fire if we died.

–Why do we have to die?

We climbed the ridge and made our way over the low rocks towards the sandy shore. But we didn't go up to where the sand was fine and ran through your fingers like the desert. We came out on the shore where the sand was firmer and beginning to be damp. Then we turned and walked down towards the sea. It looked miles away. And as we walked the sand became wetter and wetter and then it was the old wood shape again with the curly stripes and after a while you couldn't keep from walking on water. Then I heard the sound of the sea getting nearer and soon you could see the wee white blobs of water dancing on the waves as they seemed to hang in the air before scooshing in to the shore and flattening out and running back again.

John said we couldn't go any further because the tide was nearly full out and it would turn soon and start to come back in and if he was down the hole he'd be drownded. I looked up at him and his chest blotted out the whole of the bathing pond behind him. I said I bet he would be able to hold the sides of the hole up with both arms and keep it from falling in. He laughed and said

–Aye, that's right, Patrick. . . .

Am I not Targa!

He took his jacket off and hung it over the shovel and rolled up his sleeves as far as they would go until his muscles were showing and he said to feel that. I felt his muscles and they were just like balls of iron or big leadies. I held his jacket and he took the shovel and began to dig a hole in the sand. As he dug he put the shovels full of sand all round the hole carefully so that they made a circular dam and kept the water from running in too much. I spotted the Glen Sannox coming across the bay, its two funnels smoking and the trail blowing behind. It got nearer and nearer and I could see the portholes bigger than I'd ever seen them before and people standing along the rail. It came up so close after a while that I thought it was going to run into Battery Point. I could hear the scoosh of the sea being cut by the bow and spraying up and the top of the funnels where there seemed to be a space before the smoke started. In front of my eyes were things I'd never seen before like ventilators and mast ropes and the captain on the bridge and people coming to look through the portholes and the flag flying out at the stern. We were so far out and it was so close up that it seemed to be sitting on top of the sea and I was looking up at it and I felt that I could put out my hand and put my finger down the funnel. The bow and Battery Point came closer and closer together and I waited for the crash but when they met, the Point stayed and the boat began to disappear, all the body slid behind, one funnel went then the other, people waved from the rails to others standing on the Point then there was the flag and the stern jutting out built high in the water, the white foam of the propellers, the seagulls following in a bunch then just the trail astern getting fainter and fainter away across the bay.

When I looked down at John the hole was up past his waist and the sand was coming up in big shovelsfull and building up around. He looked up at me and laughed and wiped his brow and said to put my hand in his pocket and I'd find a butt and a box of matches. I gave these to him and he had a smoke. While he was doing this a great big wave, bigger than any of the others, rose up and came crashing in to the shore, nearly up to the hole and John said that was the backwash from the Glen Sannox.

Then he was digging again and the hole got deeper and deeper. And the sand became blacker and blacker with each shovel full and they were coming up more slowly. Then at last it was all black and thick and sticky and this was the duff. I threw the bag down to him and he took it and placed it at the bottom to fill it but now the tide had turned and the water was getting deeper around us and beginning to trickle through the dam. I said to g'on John, g'on, the tide was coming in but he just grunted and said was he not Targa and he was shovelling the duff into the bag quicker and quicker and his muscles were standing out. But the sea was coming in more and more through the dam and I was beginning to feel frightened. I said

–Come on John, you'll get buried!

and his legs were sinking. But he worked like mad till the bag was full then he threw up the rope attached to it to me and shouted

–Grab that line sailor!

I caught the rope and held on to it and John pulled his legs slowly out of the duff, he was nearly up to his knees. He got the shovel and dug a shelf in one side then one higher up on the other. Now the water was beginning to gurgle through the dam and it rushed down the sides more and more, slowly filling the hole and bits of the dam began to crumble and fall down in with a splash. I was lying flat holding on to the rope and I was dead scared and I felt like you do in the pictures when the good yin is getting nearer and nearer to the circular saw and nothing can save him. John threw the shovel up out of the hole. Then he got one foot up on one of the shelves and supported himself with his arms. He gradually moved his other foot up to the shelf on the other side and now the wall was crumbling and collapsing all round him and the bag was sinking too. But he hauled himself up on to the other shelf then kicked in again above and with his legs spreadeagled across the hole, managed to get to the top and flung himself over. Then straightaway he grabbed the rope and said

–Come on squareshoulders, get Silver King on the end of this rope!

We began to haul with all our strength and the bag gave a loud suck and same up slowly and John grabbed it when it got near the top and pulled it up himself and swung it round, well away from the hole.

We watched the hole caving in and filling up and the tide was coming in faster. John said

–Targa escapes again in the nick of time!

And I looked up at him and I thought he was great. He said we'd better hurry or we would be cut off, putting his jacket on and slinging the bag of duff up on his back, and away we went towards the boat on top of the spire on the English Church away in the distance, me carrying the shovel. Water seeped through the bag and ran down his back as he walked.

When we got to the steps leading up to Arran Place, John put the bag down at the top and said I was to stand guard over it with my gun at the ready while he went for the barrow. So I pulled out my tin gun that fires caps and took up my position behind the bag in case there were any bad yins about or Indians or Academy mugs.

After a while he came back with the station barrow. You just go into the railway goods yard and take this barrow if nobody has taken it first and when you're finished you bring it back and nobody will say a word to you or check you.

–All clear?

–All clear!

I stuck the gun back in my galluses and John swung the bag of duff on to the barrow and pushed off and I walked along beside him, holding on to one of the handles and singing as we were going.

–Oh, the bonny wee barrow's mine,
It didnae belong tae O'Hara!
But the fly wee joke,
He stuck t' the rope,
And I'm gonna stick tae the barrow!

Down Arran Place past the English Church and the old grey deserted house with all the weeds growing behind the gates and the cement lion smiling at us as we went past. As we came through the station gates and turned into Bute Place a crowd was coming along Princes Street. Men with caps and mufflers and some with just brass shirt studs shining were marching along in lines carrying placards, some of them playing mouthamoniums and some of them beating on an old drum. They were followed by women and men and a lot of boys and lassies. They turned into Bute Place in front of us and stopped outside the Good Templars Hall.

–What's the band, John?

–It's not a band, it's the Hunger Marchers.

I asked him if I could stay and watch them and he said all right, he'd take the duff up but I was to stay on the edge of the crowd or I'd get squashed. Jimmy McAteer was outside his coalhouse and he called

–Hullo Hamish! Ye mauna tramp the Scotch thistle, lauddie!
–What y' saying?
–A.1. soap powder.
–Are you g'on to watch the Hunger Marchers?
–Aye, come on you can stand up with me on our wash-house window.

He helped me up on the window sill and I could see over the heads of the crowd. A man got up on a chair. He was wearing grey flannels and you could see his knees through the cloth. A bit of his shirt was sticking out through a hole in the back of his trousers and when he spoke the brass stud moved up and down on his Adam's apple. He put his hands up above his head.

–All together now!
One, two, three, four,
Who are we for?
We're for the Working Class,
To *hell* with the Ruling Class!

The crowd all chanted it together then cheered at the end.

–Hullaw!

I said to James

–Will they all go down below for saying the word that means the Bad Fire?
–Unless they go to confession in time.

The crowd began to shout again.

–We want bread!
Give us work!
Let us live!
Good old Paddy!

James said that was Paddy Flanagan up on the chair. If they try to stop their burroo money he fights their case. I asked him what was their case. He said he didn't know.

–Our weans are starving!
Give us boots!

Somebody got a big piece of cloth coloured red and two of them held it above their heads.

–Workers of the world, unite!
. . . to lose . . . your chains!
I asked Jimmy if he meant their watch chains or the chains you pull in the closet. He said no, it meant the change you get back in the shop when you go for the messages, if you lose it your mammy will murder you.
–Here's the polis!
The crowd began to scatter in all directions at once and Paddy Flanagan shouted
–Close the ranks!
A polisman came round Harbour Place corner and another round the bank corner and the crowd of people were running away as fast as their legs could carry them but Paddy and all the men with the knees coming through their trousers formed into lines again and stood with their heads up. The polis stood nearhand, watching them. Some of the crowd still hung about in bunches and they started to shout at the polis.
–Leave them alone!
Let us live!
Go and catch the big bugs up the shore!
. . . the grocers in the jail for giving short weight!
Put the swindlers in the burroo behind bars!
Who put the blind woman out on the cold stones!
Paddy Flanagan turned to his men. His shirt was sticking out through a hole in his trousers. On the ground he was a very wee man with bowly legs.
–Workers, are you ready?
–Yes!
–Put up the banner!
Two men held the piece of red cloth above their heads.
–All together!
One, two, three, four,
Who are we for?
We're for the Working Class,
To *hell* with the Ruling Class!
Then they turned and with Paddy Flanagan at their head,

the ten men marched away towards Princes Street, some playing mouthamoniums, some clanking soup spoons, one banging the old drum and all singing.

–Hullaw for Nellie!
Hullaw for Dan!
Hullaw for Jock!
And hullaw for Tam!
For we'll rally round the flag boys,
We'll rally once again,
Shouting out the battle cry of freee-*dom*!

I felt a tingling up and down my back and I saw on the Hunger Marchers the uniforms of the U.S. Cavalry as they marched up Bute Place through the smoke of battle, some of them wounded, with the piano playing the battle music and shots in the distance, the tattered banner flying and Paddy Flanagan leading his soldiers on although he knew it was a losing battle but they were not going to run away or be beat.

Jimmy said

–Are you coming down the Bath Rocks for a stiff yin?

–No, there's a game of football through the Big Pen, are you coming?

–No, I have to split the sticks.

I jumped down off the window and put on my U.S. Cavalry uniform. I climbed up on the back of Silver King and, drawing my sword from its scabbard, I charged through the polis, hacking right and left. When I got to the Big Pen I jumped off and tied Silver King to the clothes pole.

We picked the teams. I was to play Inside Left and we could only get a wee round green rubber ball. It wasn't the size of tuppence but it was the biggest we could get.

In the middle of the game there were five men between me and the goal and suddenly the wee green ball was in front of me. Without stopping I kicked it on the run, aiming through the legs of the other team's backie who was in front of me. I didn't get much strength behind the kick because I didn't get it full on but the ball rolled between the backie's legs as I had wanted it to. It kept on rolling and it seemed to go slowly through a crowd of players and the goalie watched it kind of hypnotised until it was through the posts.

–Goal!

All the team gathered round and slapped me on the back. I thought I heard other voices and, looking up at the attic window, I saw m'mammy, m'daddy and John laughing and waving to me. I felt great when I knew they had seen me score the goal and that turned out to be the winning goal. We beat them three to two.

When I got up the stairs m'daddy said

–Are you going to be another Patsy Gallagher, wee fella? Is that what you're going to be? Or a Jimmy McGrory maybe it is you will be. . . . Ah, but Jimmy has the power, you know. . . . It's them wee soft ones that beat them. . . . That's how Patsy used to score his goals. . . . He would slip them in when no-one was lookin' . . . right through their legs . . . like the one you scored. . . .

–Who did Patsy Gallagher play for, daddy?

–Sure, didn't I tell you? . . . He played for the great Celtic. . . .

–Are Celtic a good team?

–A good team? There's no team can touch them. . . . It's the greatest team in the world. . . . None can hold a candle to them. . . . The great Glasgow Celtic. . . . Aye. . . . Maybe you'll play for Celtic when you grow up. . . .

–What colour are their jerseys, daddy?

–Green and white stripes. . . . Aye, the oul' green and white. . . . They're hangin' men and women for the wearin' o' the green!

When I grow up I'll play Inside Left for the greatest team in the world, Celtic, and I'll score the winning goal in the Cup Final. I'll ride up to the ground on Silver King and I'll always wear two guns and they'll call me the Celtic Kid.

The duff that John dug up had been squeezed into lumps and they were all drying on the hob until they would be hard balls then they would be burned in the fire because there wasn't any coal and that was all we had.

17

The last school day before the summer holidays we went in a new motor bus with THE STAR painted on it and a door at the side instead of the back. This bus is not Mick Kelly's, it's owned by the Cunninghams. Micky runs the green Morris to school but if you go in this one you get a free cigarette card with your ticket. You don't even get a ticket on Mick Kelly's bus. I'm saving them up. FILM STARS. I've got Laura La Plante, William Haines, Edmund Lowe, Stewart Rome, Coleen Moore, Ramon Novarro who I want to look like when I grow up, Janet Gaynor and Charles Farrel, Warner Oland, Lon Chaney, Victor McLaglen, Ken Maynard, Tim McCoy, Fatty Arbuckle, Noah Beery.

We all had on our best jerseys and a tie and polished boots and our hair flattened down with water and only a roll for playtime because we would get away early. We didn't have any lessons to do but the teacher gave us picture books to look at and she kept going through the partition to talk to the other teacher in the next class. Every time she turned her back I played blank or a face cigarette cards with the boy in the seat beside mine. When I covered the cards in my hand he kept saying three a blank or two a face, changing from one to the other. But I just kept saying three a blank every time without changing and at the end I won fifteen off him.

There was the sound of feet scraping on the floor and desk lids being banged down then the teacher came back from the partition and told us all to line up, the girls in one row and the boys in the other. We marched out through a porch, across the playground and into the Advanced Division class room. Partitions had been pulled back on both sides to make three classrooms into one. We sat down near the front. The headmaster came in and the teacher said to stand and we stood then she said to sit and we sat. The headmaster made a speech then he started giving out the prizes. A bell rang and me and my pals all shouted

–The bell, the bell,
The B-I-L,
Twenty minutes past twelve!

We went home along the shore and showed each other our prizes and chased across the grass and pulled each other down and shouted that we didn't have to go back to school for eight weeks hullaw, and we skipped and jumped and even the silver fish were doing the shimmy on the sea again because the sun was shining and we had got away.

18

It was time for the farmers to lift up the tatties and the tattie-howkers had come to howk them out. They come over from Ireland on the Belfast Boat and live in bothys near the farms. They look like gypsies, the men with coloured scarves round their necks and the women, coloured cloths on their heads and you can't make out what they're saying when they speak. I asked my daddy if they were from Belfast and he said not at all, they were a lot of oul' yokels from the shugh!

We had all got bags as big as we could get, some had message bags and we were going up the country in a gang to get tatties. Marching along we sang

–Wha saw
The tattie-howkers?
Wha saw
Them gang awa'
Wha saw
The tattie-howkers
Marching through
The Fenian Raw!

Annie and me, Margit Morgan, Mary McFarlane, Lizzie Boyle, Robert and Josie Cook, Alec and Robert Taylor all going along together. The McGraws were on the road too and some of the Fenian Row Gang but we kept away from them as the lassies said they were always fighting and they would be frightened.

–Some of them
Had boots and stockings,
Some of them
Had nane ata'

Some of them
Had bowly legs,
When marching through
The Fenian Raw!

We turned left at the Town Cross, made our way towards the dock railings then turned right up Montgomerie Street. There was a big boat lying at the other side of the railings with a black and yellow funnel. Annie said it was called the Baron Strickland. Cranes were letting diggers clang down into the hold and they came up again full of iron ore. Then they swung the diggers round and dropped the load into wagons which were drawn up alongside. At the top of Montgomerie Street we went over the Brae, stopping to look at the Caledonian Railway where it runs into Montgomerie Street Station. Behind the station were the silver tanks of the Shell Mex Oil Refinery and beyond there, the berth where the oil tankers come in.

At the other side of the brae was the beginning of the North Shore. That is not flat like the South Beach and it doesn't have a promenade but it's wilder with sand dunes like in the pictures about the Foreign Legion and grass grows out of the tops of the dunes and there are rabbits away further along where the grass grows down to the sea. You feel more like an explorer there than you do down at the South Beach and you are glad that there is a lot of you because you would be scared if you were by yourself. I put a saddle on Silver King as soon as we got to the sand and hung the bag from the saddle horn. I was wearing my Foreign Legion uniform.

The sun was behind the clouds and you could see Arran clearly. The glens, all the mountains, wee white clouds on the side of a hill, the stream running down from Goatfell and Goatfell itself, the highest peak of all, with its tip white with snow. Margit Morgan said when we went along a bit we would be able to see the Sleeping Warrior. I asked who he was and Lizzie Boyle said I would soon see. I went ch! ch! with my mouth to make Silver King go up and down the dunes and after a while Margit said there it was.

When you looked at the whole island of Arran from one end to the other it was like a great big warrior, Robert Bruce or somebody, a giant, lying flat on his back with his hands folded on his chest. You could see his nose and his head and neck then his hands and legs even the knees and the feet sticking up at the end. I said

–I bet he could get up and paddle through the sea to Belfast!

Annie said

–No, he couldn't.

Robert Cook said

–Yes he could. My grandfather McNamee said there's one like him in Ireland called Finn MacCool and he paddled across and made the Isle of Man!

Nobody knew this one's name. I said

–I bet he gets up at night when everybody is in bed and goes for a swim. I'm going to look tonight out the attic window!

We tramped for a long way over the dunes and the grass till we came to a burn running out from the country but nobody knew the name of it. There weren't any big rocky places like the Bath Rocks down the Inches but every so often there would be great big rocks like giant stones sitting by themselves. You would never be able to climb to the top of them because they were all round and slippery and shiny. Only the seagulls could sit on top of them. A farmer had his horse and cart down near the water's edge and he was loading the cart up with wrack for his fields.

We cut in nearer to the road that runs along the shore and then we could see the tattie fields on the right over a wall. The tattie howkers were at work, shouting at each other in words that you couldn't make head or tail of like the sailors off the foreign boats. One was singing a funny song. It sounded as if he was very sad and he was going to cry. Robert Cook said

–I think he is a Ben Shee!

The lassies all squealed and shouted for their mammy and daddy and said they were not going over that wall. I said

–Och, I've got my sword and I'll cut his head off if he tries to put you in his bag!

The men had forks and they dug up the shaws and turned them over. Then the women followed and picked the potatoes off and filled them into boxes. A man then came along, collected the boxes and took them away to the farm.

We followed up behind them and rummaged through the shaws that they had already gone through. You would get a potato that had been missed here and there and that way we began to fill our bags. The farmer let us do this as long as we didn't go near the potatoes that had not been dug up.

The sun was shining, it was very warm and we worked in our bare feet. Halfway through the day we stopped picking and carried our bags into the Mill Glen near the fields. It was cool coming in under the trees out of the sun and our backs were sore from bending. Branches were gathered from in amongst the trees and the high ferns and with these we made a fire. We had got a couple of old tins from the back of the Coperative on our way up Montgomerie Street and we filled them with water from the burn that runs through the glen, that becomes the Galloway further down. We put some tatties in one of the tins and boiled them in their skins and when they were ready we stuck branches in them and ate them that way and they were hot, steamy and like balls of flour, they were that soft. They tasted even better in the Mill Glen than they did at home. After the tatties we made some tea in the other tin, putting a wee bit of stick in to keep it from getting smoked by the fire.

After that I said I was the Indian Chief and they were my braves and the lassies could be the Indian squaws. We said we had captured Buffalo Bill and we were going to burn him on the fire. Then we all danced around it singing

–Tarry-um-a-dee,
The monkey's up a tree,
Ate all the coconuts
And left nane for me!

Sometimes we jumped over the fire through the flames and this frightened the lassies and they said they would tell but we said we would brand their faces with a red hot branch so they shut up. Then we all went down to the burn and washed our faces which were all black from the smoke.

–Dan, Dan,
The funny wee man,
Washed his face
In the frying pan!

We came back up and threw water from the burn on to the fire then jumped on it to put it out and then made our way back to the tattie fields. As we climbed the hill from the Glen I looked back and you could see the clearing where we had been, the white steamy smoke still curling up from the fire through the trees.

The tattie-howkers were sitting around in the field eating pieces and drinking something from jugs, laughing and joking and singing. Then they went back to work again and we followed them and by about four o'clock we had our bags full.

When we got home with them, mammy said

–That's a fine lot of tatties you got for me, childher. Those will last a long while.

She put on the pot and gave us a plate of tatties and butter.

After we finished I heard bagpipes playing in the distance, tuning up the way they sound very sad and ghostie. I said

–Mammy, can I go and see the Pipe Band?

–Aye, away you go for being a good wee boy and getting the tatties.

I went with Robert and Josie Cook and Alec Taylor. As we went up Hill Street we passed the new black motor bus that's started. It's got ten doors all along both sides and the seats go across from one door to the other. The man that drives it wears leather leggings, a black peaked cap and goggles. He's got a round red face and a black moustache with waxed spiky ends. This bus has got a hood which folds at the back in the Summer and comes up when it's raining.

We went up the path to the Drill Hall on the Cannon

Hill and stood outside the door with a big crowd of weans. You could hear the pipers inside tuning up and the drums clattering. One of the pipers came out, went up to the corner, lifted his kilt and did a pee through the railings on to the railway lines. It was like a waterfall.

Then they all came outside the hall, somebody locked the doors and they began to line up. On the big drum it said ARDROSSAN WINTON PIPE BAND and the man carrying this looked like a giant with big deep wrinkles on his face and leopard skins on his back. They all had marvellous red tartan kilts—Stuart, John once told me—a dirk in their stockings, a sporran hanging in front of the kilt and a big cairngorm brooch on their chest. They were great, they looked like the picture of Bonnie Prince Charlie on our tea caddy and the leader was Pipe Major Dunlop. I am going to be a kiltie when I grow up and learn to play the pipes.

The pipes skirled out, the side drums rattled, the big drums boomed and they marched away with the Pipe Major twirling his stick at the head. Away we went behind, marching along, trying to keep step, down Princes Street and through the Station Gates.

Men were working on the old grey house as we went past, pounding the walls with great big hammers and knocking it down. The band marched along South Beach Road and now there were women following it and lassies and big men too.

When we reached the green the band halted then they all stood around in a ring and played the Black Bear. Someone had put down a wooden platform and one of the kilties got up on this and did the sword dance over two crossed swords and everybody went

–Hooch!

When he was finished he got a great cheer.

While I was watching, a hand touched me on the back, I turned round and it was Jimmy McAteer, he had a walking stick in his hand. I asked him where he was going and he said he was going over the shore to play at golf, was I coming? He had a ball, one of the ones that you find among the long grass on the Golf Course sometimes, and this old walking stick for a club. I asked him to give me a hit. He put the ball down on the grass, handed me the walking stick and I hit it towards the shore. When we got up to the ball, near the promenade, Jimmy Biggar who lives down the street beside Nicol's Bar and thinks he can box, had run over and picked it up and he said

–This ball is mine, I lost it over our back wall. I know by that mark on it.

–No it isn't, you're a liar. It belongs to James McAteer.

–If you call me a liar I'll punch you on the nose!

All his pals were standing round him and then my pals came up. I said

–I'm not afraid of you. That's our ball. Give it back to me.

–You're not getting it. It's mine. You'll have to fight me for it.

–Give us the ball!

–I'm keeping it.

He turned and walked away. I looked at Jimmy McAteer and he was looking at his hands. I ran after Jimmy Biggar and stood in front of him and said

–Give me that ball!

–It's my ball, get out of my way or I'll bash you.

–Try it!

My pals had come up again and some of them were saying to go on, not to let him hit me. Jimmy Biggar began to twist his lip up at the side and make a face like a boxer. He said

–Away, I wouldn't want to hit you.

–Try it!

–Do you want a fight, then?

–I'll fight you anytime.

All the boys began to shout

–Come on, here's a fight!

–Come on down the shore and fight it out!

–You can fight him, Patty!

But Alec Taylor said

–Don't fight him, Pat, he's learning to be a boxer.

And James McAteer said

–Let him keep the ball, Patrick. Come on away, don't fight him, he's bigger than you and older.

Jimmy Biggar said

–Where will we go, down the shore?

–I could fight you anywhere!

–Come on then.

The whole crowd of us went down on to the beach from the promenade and, as the tide was out, we made our way out to where the rocks of the Inches started so that no big bodies would stop us. As we went, I heard the pipe band start up again behind us and the cheers of the crowd but as we got nearer the sea the wind was stronger and began to blow the sound away and I half-wished that I was still following the band. I had the leadie taste in my mouth and I felt a bit frightened. I was wondering to myself why there had to be people like Jimmy Biggar and why he had to come along just at that time. I wished that we were all at home sitting by the fire or looking out of the window but I knew that I wouldn't draw out of it no matter what happened.

All the rest formed a ring and we, the two fighters, walked towards each other in the centre. We stopped and put our fists up and I was getting ready to circle round and spar like the boxers do in the pictures and m'daddy showed me when Jimmy Biggar rushed straight at me with his fists flying. Although I stuck my left foot out and duked about on my feet, it didn't stop him like it does in the pictures, he just came sailing right through and landed punches galore all over my face, his fists going like a windmill. One of them landed in my eye and I saw stars of all colours again, the same as when I was knocked out in the playground. Another dinged me in the ear and made it ring. Then I lost my balance and fell down.

–Let him up!

–Stand back!

–Letty up! Letty up!

When I got things straight I could see that Jimmy Biggar was standing well back, waiting for me to get up. James McAteer came forward to help me.

–No helping!

–He has to get up by himself!

I was glad they were shouting because I didn't want to be helped. I got up on my feet again and edged my way towards the centre of the ring. This time I rushed at Biggar with my fists flying but although I got a punch into his side, I couldn't get him in the face because he had his head down. My fists kept bouncing off the hard top of his head while every so often one of his fists would come sailing up and land on my nose. It took three punches before it began to bleed. Then I remembered m'daddy saying to John and me that the way to beat a bruiser who keeps his head down is to give him a good uppercut. Next time he came in with his arms flying I stepped back and brought my fist up underneath with its fullest force then I followed it up with the left, two lovely uppercuts. Biggar staggered back a bit and I could see that I had got him in the eye but he came straight back at me again and landed another punch on my ear that made it sing and knocked me down again.

When I was on the ground I heard the sound of bagpipes and I thought I was hearing things because of the clout I had taken on the ear then the sound came nearer and some of Jimmy Biggar's pals began to say

–Here's the pipe band coming back, let's go and follow it.

–Come on Jimmy, let's follow the band home!

–You've beat him anyway!

–Come on!

–Better leave him or you'll kill him!

Jimmy Biggar went over, picked up the ball again and said

–This is my ball and I'm keeping it, see!

By this time I was back on my feet and I was standing with my fists up again but he was running away over the rocks with his gang to get up the steps and follow the band. I shouted after him,

–You didn't beat me anyway!

Blood from the nose was running into my mouth, my ears were dinging and I could only see half the world. The Taylors and the Cooks went off to follow the band but James McAteer came over and put his arm round my shoulders and said

–Come on Patrick, we'll away over the Bath Rocks and find a puddle and I'll bathe your face for you.

–I didn't let him beat me, did I?

–No, you didn't let him beat you.

We went away over the rocks till we came to a puddle. James bathed my face with salt water and managed to clean most of the blood off but the bruises were beginning to come up, there was a big one on my forehead. James said if you would put a penny on that, it would go down but I hadn't got a penny. He said we'd better away home now.

We went over the Bath Rocks to go home by the Inches Road and as we were climbing down the other side I fell on to the rocks beneath. I was a bit dizzy and I couldn't see properly from the thumping I had got and I missed my foot and half slithered and half fell to the bottom. On my way down I hit my left ankle a crack on a spur of rock jutting out which made it feel kind of numb. James lifted me up and asked me if I was all right. It didn't affect me very much because I was half-groggy at the time, it was just the funny feeling in my ankle. It was some time before I could put it down and walk on it to go home. James said

–You've been in the war today, talk about Gene Tunney!

and he went in the house.

When I got home m'mammy gave me a row for fighting and asked me who it was and she would go and tell his mother. Of course I wouldn't tell her because m'daddy told me it was being an oul' sneak to tell on someone else. I told him I had given the other one an uppercut because he kept his head down and he said

–Aye, that's right son. Bring your fist up underneath and uppercut them!

He wouldn't let m'mammy get on to me any more. I had to go to bed early but m'daddy gave me a horseback and before I went under the clothes he whispered

–Who won anyway?

–I didn't let him beat me! I didn't let him beat me.

19

–An aeryplane! An aeryplane!
I heard them shouting down the backyard while I was eating a roll for my breakfast so I left it and rushed down the stairs to see. The weans all began to sing

–An aeryplane,
To watch the wean,
My mammy's in
The beershop!

I heard the engine first then saw the aeryplane itself coming over the Fenian Row chimleys.

–An aeryplane
To watch the wean!

We sang it over and over again, windows went up, heads came out and the street became filled with knots of people all looking up at the sky. It had two wings and a thing like a bullseye on each tip. I could see the propeller whirring, the struts glinting in the light and the pilot's head sticking out of the cockpit. It went out of sight from Harbour Place and a crowd of us ran round into Princes Street and, looking up Hill Street, the last thing we saw was it disappearing behind the castle on the Cannon Hill.

Josie Cook and me went back round the wee world. Passing the Union Bank of Scotland, a big toff wearing a soft hat came walking out.

–Any cigarette cards, mister?
He stopped, looked down at me, pulled out a cigarette packet and gave me the card from inside saying to run along, sonny. I shouted to Josie to look what I'd got. It was one of the set of Film Stars, William Haines.

–Has your daddy gone back to sea yet?

–No, he's still home. Wullie Brannif's home from sea.

–Is he?
–Yes. He was fighting with the Polis last night. He threw two of them over his head. He was great.
–He's a great fighter, isn't he?
–Yes, he could beat anybody.
–I was fighting yesterday.
–Who with?
–Jimmy Biggar.
–Hey, he's a boxer, isn't he?
–Yes, he's a champion.
–Who won?
–No-one. I didn't let him beat me.

Going down Bute Place, my ankle felt funny again. Josie asked me to play at bools but I didn't feel like it. I went in and I told m'mammy that my left ankle felt funny and how I got it. She let me sit on the chair and play on the table or look out of the window for the rest of the day.

After a few days it felt worse and I could hardly walk on it. I was wingeing a bit with the pain and m'mammy sent John out with m'daddy's Sunday boots—John whispered to me it was to the pawnshop—and when he came back with some money she took us all to the pictures. John had to carry me all the way, there and back.

Doctor McCann came the next day and he said I had to go to bed and stay there. I couldn't put it on the ground anymore.

On Thursday it began to swell till it was up like a balloon and when Doctor McCann came he said that I would have to go into hospital straight away. He said he would arrange for me to go in and my mother would have to take me up on the train to Glasgow on Saturday.

20

–Patrick, you're a villain!
Patrick, you're a rogue!
There's nothing of you Irish,
Except your name and brogue.
Ah, you're killing me by inches,
You know I am your slave.
But when you're dead
You mean old scut,
I'll dance upon your grave!

It was Saturday morning and m'daddy was singing this to me as he often did while I was getting washed and dressed. I was trying to laugh but the pain in my ankle was very bad and it was all swollen up so that I could hardly make out the shape of my foot. I had to keep it propped up on a chair when I wasn't in bed. M'mammy had on her good costume and John had his Sunday suit, a collar and tie and a cap.

When I was ready, m'daddy gave me a penny and said

–Cheerio, wee fella, I'll come and see you soon.

I said so long to Annie then we went off to the station, John carrying me on his back. We didn't have far to go, just down Bute Place to the station gates.

While mammy bought tickets and spoke to the ticket clerk, John went inside with me and waited. We had a look at the machine that prints your name for a penny and the chocolate machine and the machine with the Puffing Billy in a glass case. Then we went and looked into the bookstall window at the books of different colours up for show to read on the trains. John read them out to me. Edgar Wallace, William Le Quex, Saki, Bruce Graeme, Sax

Rohmer, A. J. Cronin, Gilbert Frankau, Sexton Blake, Dixon Hawke, Sherlock Holmes, Doctor Fu Manchu.

The train was leaving from platform number one. The railwayman taking the tickets said

–Good morning, Missus O'Connor, is your wee boy not well?

–No, Mister Neill, he's got a poisoned ankle and we're taking him to the hospital. You won't want anything for him, will you?

–Well . . .

–He's being carried.

–Och, no. Go on, sure he's only a wean anyway. Tell them that in Glasgow.

–Right Mister Neill. I'm behoulden to you!

–Not a bit of it. I hope you get on all right with the wee boy. Ta-ta the now!

We got into the train and sat waiting for it to go. A pug went by on the other line going to the harbour and it was pulling wagons of iron ore and wagons of stooky, some of them covered with oilskins.

–Look Patrick, there's some covered wagons!

–Yes.

–We never saw one of them in the pictures, did we?

–No.

The train blew its whistle and pulled out. I wasn't taking much notice on the way because the pain was hurting me so much but John told me the stations as we went past. Ardrossan South Beach, Saltcoats, Stevenston, Kilwinning, Dalry, Beith, Lochwinnoch, Milliken Park, Elderslie, Johnstone, Paisley Canal. Then there was a different noise to all the other stations and it was Glasgow Saint Enoch's. There seemed to be a lot of railway barrows clattering and carriage doors slamming, train whistles sounding, trains starting up and it was all echoing as if we were in the canyon down the Bath Rocks.

When we got out of the train I looked up and there was this great big glass roof over everything, miles up in the air with giant steel girders keeping it all up. There were trains on both sides, stretching away into the distance and umpteen platforms. Going through the gate, the ticket man looked over his glasses.

–Is your wee boy sick?

–Yes, we're going to the hospital.

–Aye, away ye go through hen . . .

We came into a big space at the end of the platforms about ten times as big as our station. There were glass-panelled doors everywhere, umpteen machines and a monster cannon shell standing in the middle that you put pennies in for something. High above was a great big long window with a man inside, walking up and down and putting up the next train to wherever it was going, the time it went out and the platform number. We turned round a corner, went down a stair with iron strips on it and out into a side street past an old woman selling Swan Vestas matches and mammy said we were in Argylle Street. You could hear the jang of tramcars. It was the first time I had seen one and they were beezers, round at both ends, blue ones, green ones, yellow ones, red ones, white ones, a man standing in a wee cabin at the front driving with a big brass handle like you use for winding up a motor, only it was standing up straight. John said you knew what tram to get by the different colours. We got on a purple one and I forgot my pain for a while, looking at everything new. Big long wooden seats along both sides, people standing hanging on to straps, the tram windows with wee coloured panes at the top, the conductor in a green uniform with silver buttons, all the different streets going past and all the motor cars and horse-and-carts. I asked John if Glasgow was a city and he said yes it was a big one. The pain was hurting again and I had to sit down from the window. I didn't look at anything but could only hear the newspaper-sellers crying.

I saw the masts of a ship sticking up over a building then we got off the tram and John put me on his back again and we walked up a steep, cobbled brae. Then through a big gate, up a drive and into the hospital. When the doors opened and closed behind us I heard heels clicking along corridors and a smell the same as just before Mary went away in her white box.

A funny woman with her hair done in an Eton Crop that made her look like a man, and wearing a white wrapper with tubes—for sounding you, John told me—sticking out of the top pocket, came and took my mammy into an office while John and I sat down to wait outside. They came out with a nurse, lifted me on to a big go-chair, trundled it down a corridor and into a room. The Eton Crop woman—Lady Doctor said John—looked at my ankle and poked. It hurt. I was X-Rayed. We sat in a room waiting then the lady doctor came in with big films and held them up to the light. She spoke quietly to my mother but I heard her say the words diseased bone in the ankle. They put me on the big go-chair again. I felt as if I was being kidnapped and I looked back for mammy and John but they said they were not going yet, they would see me in the ward. The nurse took me into a room with other nurses, lifted me and sat me in a chair. They took all my clothes off without turning away and I got a red face as they could see my teapot. Then they put me into a big bath and washed me. It was very hot but in the water my foot didn't hurt so much. When I was dried, another nurse with a different hat combed my hair the opposite way from the way it usually gets combed and that made me feel all wasted. Then they put me in a kind of nightgown tied with tapes at the side, then on to a trolley and I went off on my travels again, along a corridor, up in a lift then into a room with only one bed in it. After I was put in between the sheets, I lay feeling my ankle jumping with the pain then John and m'mammy came in. She had the same look on her face that she has when she is looking at a sad picture or when someone is not well and she wants to help them and her eyes were a bit watery.

–Is it hurting you, son?

–No, not much.

–You'll soon be better son, and we'll come and take you home.

–Tell James McAteer I'm all right.
–Aye son, I'll tell his mother when I'm speaking to her.
–Will you keep Silver King in the stable for me, John, and see he gets plenty of hay?
–I will. Am I not Targa?

I felt they were going to go away then and the pain was jumping and I was trying with all my might not to cry. My throat was getting dry and the feeling was coming over me but I was gripping the bedclothes tight underneath and scringeing my teeth hard. A nurse came in and whispered something then they came over to me. I was swallowing for all I was worth and nearly tearing holes in the bedclothes under me.

–We'll have to away now, son. We'll come up and see you soon. Next Saturday.
–Will you bring me some comics and the *Startler?*

That's the book with Targa the Terrible in it and that daft fella called Green as Grass.

–Yes, we will.
–And my bools and a game?
–Yes, all right.

They came over to the bed and leaned over.

–Ta-ta son . . .
–So long Patrick.

M'mammy bent down and gave me a hug then John gripped me by the shoulder. I couldn't look at them as they went out the door.

–Ta-ta son . . .
–T—

I heard their footsteps fading away down the corridor and then the nurse coming back alone. I scringed my teeth again.

–Does it hurt?
–Aye, it's sort of jumping.

She went to a trolley and got some pills. She said to take these, I swallowed them and washed them down with water. She told me to lie down, tucked me in and went away.

The tears came slowly and filled my eyes up like puddles then dripped down on to the pillow. My chest began to shake and I felt as if I wanted to squeeze something out of me, my face all screwed up, then the tears came quicker and I was girning buckets. It wasn't fair that I should be left alone here, miles from home, while John and my mother went away back on the train and daddy was sitting by the fire telling Annie a story. They would be going out the gates now and down the cobbled hill.

Rain began to spatter on the window. It was very still and quiet in the room by myself and I cried for a long time until the day began to fade and I fell asleep.

21

When I awoke next day I was in a ward with other children. It was not yet daylight and two nurses were going round, one shaking us up and another handing us a cup of porridge and milk with a spoon to eat it. We were hardly finished when another came around collecting the empty cups, followed by another two making the beds. After that we were washed from a basin at the bedside and our hair combed. Dawn was breaking as I was just dropping off to sleep again while sitting up when I was shaken awake again and someone walked down the ward shouting

–Feeders and serviettes!

These were dished out then someone came around with trays filled with bread and margarine cut into half slices. We ate this with a half-cup of milk. That was breakfast every morning, I was told by the boy in the next bed, unless your family brought you eggs. Then you had to watch them for the nurses would pinch one for themselves. One boy must have been the son of big bugs because he had an egg every morning and the nurses were always making a fuss of him. He also had chocolate biscuits and bananas and oranges. If you weren't a big bug, you were hungry all the time, this boy in the next bed said.

In the middle of the ward there was a big long table with flowers on it. Around the table there were pedal motor cars, tricycles, swings, scooters and wooden railway engines. Around these there was a red coloured rope and nobody was allowed to go under the rope and use the toys. A nurse sat at a table writing and she had to keep getting up and shoving away the children who thought they could play on the toys.

Out the window across the yard you could see cranes

and factories and what looked like the deckwork of boats in a dock. There was nothing outside the window behind except green grass in front of another building. You could sometimes see nurses moving through the windows and the backs of beds and sometimes a bandaged head so it must have been another ward.

My ankle was hurting terrible so I told one of the nurses and she gave me some more pills. On one side of me was an empty bed and on the other a boy with dark curly hair like the Angel Gabriel. His name was Bobby, he said. A boy who was allowed to get up came over and asked me if I would like to play a game of Ludo. But my ankle was jumping all the time and I couldn't think of anything else. After a bit I began to feel sleepy and I drifted off with the sounds of the ward getting fainter.

–Feeders and serviettes!

I woke up with a jump. A lassie—an up-patient as they were called—was giving them out. Then everybody shouted

–Here's dinner!

Nurses came around carrying trays on which were tin plates of mince with a blob of champed tatties on the side and a spoon to eat it with. It took about half-a-jiffy to eat that then everybody shouted

–Here's pudding!

You licked the spoon used for the mince and tatties and ate the pudding with it. That was half-a-cup of custard so thin, you didn't need a spoon, you just drank it out of the cup. That was dinner finished. I wasn't feeling very hungry because of the pain but I asked the boy in the next bed if he was hungry and he said you always felt hungry in here. I asked him what they got yesterday and he said mince and tatties, you got mince and tatties every day and one day you got half-a-cup of pudding after and the next day half-a-cup of soup before.

Sometime after dinner my pain got worse and somebody called a sister, pushed in a trolley with bottles and tubes on it and stuck a needle in my leg. After a while it got kind of numb and the pain went away.

There was a wee tin gramophone called a kiddiphone. Someone put a record on it and a man with a cracked voice sang

–All among the barley,
Sitting supping soup!

Then I played Ludo with one of the up-patients then it was tea-time and we got half-slices of toast and a wee bit of cheese.

After the tea two nurses came and took away the empty bed and returned soon with someone in it, a girl with her head covered in bandages like a turban. She had a funny, croaking voice and was always crying.

The evening came and you could see lights coming on in the factory windows and strings of street lamps and the shadows in the ward got darker. Most of the lamps in the ward were put out then two nurses came around with a trolley, gave us all a cup of hot milk and tucked us in for the last time. Then all the lights were out and we were told to go to sleep. It got quieter and darker and you could hear some snoring here and there. My ankle wasn't hurting that much anymore and it was not long before I fell asleep also.

–Nurse!
Nurse!
There's a man behind the curtains!
He's got a hatchet!
He's going to split my head open!

I thought I was having nightmares then I found I was awake and the screams and shouts were coming from the girl with the bandaged head in the next bed. She had got out from under the clothes and was down at the bottom of the bed, coorying in a corner. Nurses came rushing down and a light was switched on over her bed. She looked as if she was frightened to death as she pointed at the curtain behind her bed. In the dark I could see other boys and lassies sitting up and my ankle began to jump again and hurt badly.

–He's behind the curtain!
I saw him!

He's got a big hatchet!

The nurses were telling her to shush and one said to look there was nobody there and pulled back the curtain.

–He must be hiding because he saw you coming!

–Sh, sh, never mind. Nobody is going to hurt you. Lie down and go to sleep. . . .

One of them brought a hot drink and some pills but she wouldn't take them. They said to come on, she would have to get back under the clothes but she wouldn't go. She kept shouting about the man with a hatchet who was hiding behind the curtains. I was hoping that he hadn't slipped behind my curtains and was waiting to spring out on me after the nurses had gone.

She wouldn't lie down or keep quiet and she kept trying to jump out of the bed. They got rolls of bandages, bound them round her wrists and tied her hands to the bed rail at each side. Then they did the same to her ankles and tied her feet to the bottom of the bed. She screamed blue murder for the rest of the night and nobody could get any sleep. My ankle was hurting like anything and I had to listen to her shouts in my ear all night but I didn't want to say anything about it as the nurses were not in a very good mood. I didn't want them to tie me to the bed as well in case the man with the hatchet came back.

I was groggy when dawn broke and the nurses came around with the half-cups of porridge and milk. They wouldn't give me any. I said to the nurse that I hadn't got any porridge and she said I was not to get any today and went away quickly. I wondered what I had done last night to deserve this. I must have done something but instead of tying me to the bed they were going to starve me.

I was washed and the bed was made, then the half-slices of bread and margarine came around.

–Nurse, I'm hungry.

–You're not to get any, O'Connor.

When it came to dinner time the mince and tatties came round and they smelt lovely. I asked for some and again I didn't get any. I just sat up in bed and smelt the mince and watched everybody eating around me and I was starving hungry. By this time the daft girl in the next bed was fast asleep and nobody woke her up.

As well as being starving, I had no sleep and my ankle was hurting worse than it had ever been. When I put my hand down to touch it, the skin felt tight and glistening and it was sore to the touch. I made up my mind that I was not going to let any of the rotten-faced nurses see me cry. I slipped down under the clothes and tried to shut out the pain.

There were sounds around me, the day faded. Food was brought round and I wasn't given any. I wondered how long I could live without food. I wondered how long they were going to starve me. Maybe they were going to starve me to death. But they would never make me cry.

Just after dusk two nurses came into the ward pushing a long trolley. It drew up beside me. They took off my grey sleeping suit and gave me a red one to put on. It was like a tent. Then the side of the cot was let down and I was lifted on to the trolley and covered with a blanket. They pushed me out of the ward. Only Bobby saw me go and he said ta-ta. I asked the nurses where we were going and one of them said

–You'll find out.

The other said

–The theatre.

They looked at each other and laughed and I could tell that the joke was on me but I didn't know what it was. I hear m'daddy speaking about the Alhambra Theatre in Belfast and the great comedians he had seen there and I knew there were theatres in Glasgow but I couldn't believe they were taking me there. They were making fun of me.

We passed down a lot of corridors and turned corners and then entered a lift and went down slowly, watching the floors passing.

–Nurse, will I see comedians in this theatre?

–Well, you might see some stars!

They both had a great laugh at this then the lift stopped. The trolley was pushed out, we went round a corner then through a door but before going through, I saw a lighted sign saying THEATRE and now I didn't know whether to believe them or not. They pushed the trolley into a corner and left me. There was a noise like a motor engine when you hear it in the distance. I felt kind of groggy and I was starving.

My heart gave a jump and I nearly felt my hair standing on end when I saw a figure coming through the doorway towards me. It was dressed completely in green, a long gown down to the floor, a green cap and a green mask over its face. The eyes were staring at me. It was the Phantom of the Louvre or maybe Doctor Mabuse. I cringed under the blankets. He took hold of the trolley and wheeled it through another door. Inside this room several members of the gang were standing looking at me as I came in. They were all dressed exactly the same in green. All wore masks. Only their eyes gleamed at me. In the centre of the room was a tall granite slab like an altar. The top was flat and smooth and there were gutterings along the side like on our roof outside the attic. A pillow on the end.

I was lifted and stretched out on this altar. The green figures crowded round. I tried to shout for help but my tongue was sticking to the roof of my mouth and nothing would come out. I was to be the sacrifice. They would offer me as sacrifice to Moloch and when I was dead they would all raise their arms and shout. Fire and smoke would belch out of Moloch's mouth and nobody would ever see me again.

But it wasn't fair, there were too many of them, I couldn't fight them all. And I was weak and starving and I didn't have any sleep. One of them gripped my left arm and another, my right. One came over close to me and looked into my eyes. A strong light above me shone straight down into them but faintly all around I could make out rubber tubes and shining silver instruments. Again I tried to shout out but found myself unable to. I tried to speak. I wanted to ask them what I had done, why didn't they leave me alone, why they were going to sacrifice me. I wanted to say it wasn't fair. Letty up. You have to let a man get up. You musn't hit him while he is lying on his back. My voice wouldn't work. No sound came. I couldn't even speak, never mind shout for help.

I thought I made out from a long distance away the trundling jang of a tramcar. If only I could be sitting in it now with John beside me. If only John was here. Was he not Targa? John would come up from Ardrossan with Wullie Brannif and the two of them would beat all those green hooded figures. They were too far away. Outside was help. The tramcar. No voice came.

The one who had looked into my eyes and gone away returned with a round gauze thing in a wire muzzle like they put on greyhounds. In it was a kind of pad of cotton wool or something. He lifted a bottle from the trolley and poured something on to the pad. A voice told me to close my eyes and start counting slowly.

The pad was over my face and the gauze was being held there. It burned. I was being choked. I wanted to vomit. Why was I being killed? I was being slowly suffocated. And they hadn't even told me what I had done wrong.

I began to struggle and lash out with my feet. To try to get my arms free. I wasn't going to die without a struggle. But I was slowly choking. Choking. I struggled more and the mesh was pressed more firmly down on my face.

The lights began to spin, the green faces went round and round me, the mad eyes glinted then the man with the hatchet jumped down from the lights and split my head open.

22

I was breathing. The air seemed colder than usual, colder even than in the winter time. I opened my eyes slowly. There was a nozzle in front of my mouth and nose. This was attached to a long rubber tube and that ran into a big steel tin. I was breathing in the cold air from the nozzle. In front of me were two swinging doors with glass panels in them.

I heard footsteps running down a corridor. They came nearer and nearer and got louder and louder then a matron burst through the doors. She came rushing up to me, bent down over my face then turned to the nurse who was holding the nozzle and said in a loud, shaky voice

–You stupid girl, I thought you said he was dead!

She looked as if she had been cheated at bools or cigarette cards.

23

The blue and black funnels of the big boats seemed to be quite close now. They were lying in the docks at the bottom of a hill which was covered with streets and houses. Some of us had our beds pulled out on to a balcony because the sun was shining. I screwed up my eyes to try and see the names on the side but they were too far away. I asked a nurse where those boats sailed to and she said India or Japan, she thought. I wouldn't mind going on a boat like that when I grow up.

I was just beginning to get an appetite two weeks after the operation and I was hoping that the mince and tatties would come round soon. M'mammy had brought me three eggs on Saturday but I only had one and I couldn't tell what happened to the other two. My ankle was itching like mad and when I managed to get my foot up and slide some of the bandages off to give it a scratch I saw that inside was all dried bloody and it was laced up like a football and a funny shape, not like the other one.

After we had our mince and tatties, the beds were wheeled back into the ward then we got an extra wash and tidy because this was the day the delegates came round. It was the only day that the up-patients could play on the big toys. The rope was taken away and they were allowed to go on the pedal motors and the wooden railway engines and toy see-saw and the nurses would push them up and down the ward while the delegates, who were all dressed in swanky clothes and fur coats and all had big round red swelling faces, looked at them and smiled and stuck their fingers in their waistcoat pockets or the women gathered the furs round their necks and patted a head here and there. They would come around the beds and ask each one of us if we were happy and the ward sister was standing beside them and looking at us and we knew if we didn't say we were happy that we might be tied to the bed with bandages or not given anything to eat for a long time.

About half-an-hour after the delegates went away the ward sister came in and all the big toys were taken back to the centre of the ward and roped off. They wouldn't come out until the delegates came round again.

On a table in the ward behind the big toys, a book was kept with all our names in it. Sometimes an Irish nurse would look at it when the sister wasn't there and tell us who was marked down to go home. One day she said

–Patrick O'Connor to go home on Saturday!

I thought she was taking a fiver out of me as this nurse was always kidding the weans on but she said no, it was as true as God should strike her down dead so I knew it must be true.

On Saturday morning after breakfast the nurses came with my clothes and put a screen round the bed and began to dress me after I had a wash. It was still painful to put my left foot on the ground and when it came to putting my boots on, the left one wouldn't go because the foot was swollen up so much and when I tried to walk it felt as if a bone was coming right through the skin on the sole of my foot. They had to just put the boot on without lacing it. After saying so long to the rest of the weans in the ward, the nurses held me on both sides and helped me down a corridor and into a room where my mother was waiting. She got up and came towards me and gave me a cuddle then helped me into a chair. The pain was terrible and my face was all screwed up trying to bear it. She looked at me and her eyes got all watery and she began to tut, tut, tut and hum and haw.

The Doctor with the Eton Crop came in and mammy and her stood facing each other. M'mammy was angry and her face was getting redder.

– . . . like a skeleton . . . must have been starved. . . .

The lady doctor stuck her hands in both pockets and said
–You're lucky to have him out at all . . . touch and go. . . .
–But look at his foot . . . and his wee face . . . wee soul can hardly walk. . . .
–You should be pleased that we didn't have it cut off . . . it was considered. . . .
–He can hardly walk on it. . . . Look at the pain he's in. . . .
– . . . It all takes time . . . time to mend. . . .

They argued for a while and m'mammy got angrier and said a few bloodies then the lady doctor suddenly turned on her heel with her face bright red and marched away. A nurse came and helped me to the door of the hospital. Then we were outside and, with me leaning on m'mammy's arm, we made our way down the long drive and out into the street and down the brae. Every time I put my left foot to the ground the pain shot up right through me. The ankle wouldn't bend and I had to shuffle it along sideways with the toes turned out. M'mammy said she was sorry John couldn't come because he was doing a wee job but if she had known I was as bad as this she would have brought him just the same.

At last we got into the tramcar and m'mammy said
–Come on my wee son, I'll take you for a good feed . . . Sure you look half starved. . . .

The tram stopped at a place called The Saltmarket and we got out and turned round a corner and you could smell the boiled cabbage a mile away. We went into THE WORKING MAN'S EATING HOUSE that had sawdust on the floor and a great big brown dumpling on a plate on the counter. We sat on wooden forms at a scrubbed table and had a good plate of cabbage, ham and tatties and after that a big slice of the brown dumpling on the counter and I fairly smallicked it up, I felt as if I had been living on a desert island with nothing to eat for years. Then we caught the train and John was at the station at home to meet us. He said

–Hullo, Green as Grass. Am I not Targa!
and lifted me up and swung me on to his back.

–Silver King will take you home across the saddle, as you have been shot in the leg.

I put on my U.S. Marshal's uniform and we went home at a canter and my daddy's eyes were crinkly when he saw me and Annie's face had a wee half smile and she had got a bit bigger and I was glad to get back to the attic and lie on the big bed and stretch my leg out and listen to the wind whistling up the chimley and the waves splashing over the Bath Rocks and the horn of a boat that would be going away out to sea sounding from the harbour.

PART II

I

Doh, re, mi, when I was wee
I used to peel the tatties.
Now I'm big and I can dig
And I can chase the lassies.

Standing on the spot I used to stand upon a lot when I was just a kid, I looked out the attic window at the waves coming in and the boats on the Firth beyond and, of course, the Bath Rocks where I had never been away from at one time and fell off once. Now I was running with the big boys and didn't need a chair anymore to help me look over the window sill. And I was in the Harbour Place gang. We had battled with the Kilmahew Street gang only the week before and beat them.

I was wearing a new pair of cordy roys and best brown boots and my broad-striped knitted tie and my stomach was in knots and I was shaking inside because we were going away on the Belfast Boat that night. But that wasn't the only reason why my stomach was in knots. I had to see James McAteer before I left that night. He knew the answer to The Question. He said he had solved The Mystery but I only half-believed him. The mystery of where we came from and how did we get here?

I had never altogether taken it in that I came down the chimley which is what m'mother always said when I asked her where I came from when I was born. I might have half-believed it when I was a wean. It's a good story all right. I used to like to try and imagine how it would feel, lying in that big cloth with the wind whistling past you as you sailed through the sky, looking up at those great wings beating above you and all the stars around as the bird headed for our attic. But then—the chimley—all that soot—the fire. No, you couldn't . . . but . . . still and all. . . .

Only Annie and m'mother and me were going on the Belfast Boat. Without much to eat for a long time, we were all getting thinner and John was never away from the pawnshop. We were lucky if we got a fish supper on a Friday night even and I had heard m'mother crying and saying to the old fella that she couldn't go on any longer, she couldn't feed the family on nothing and there was no work to be had anywhere.

Then m'father's sister, Aunt Annie had written from Derry where she has a sweetie shop saying she would take the three of us over for the Summer holidays but John and himself could stay on over here and maybe find a job. M'mother and Annie were to help in the shop. She had sent the fares as well. It was a Godsend m'mother said. My auntie was trying to get a shop started in Buncrana forbye, not as high-class as the one in Derry and we would be living there too for a while, in Donegal. At last I would see Belfast where my mother and father both came from and which I had been hearing about since the proverbial chimley happening. And I would see my eldest sister, Bridget, who I had hardly ever laid eyes on because she was already living with Auntie and helping in the shop and before that had always been away from home working as a maid in big swanky houses.

So I was in a right confloption, standing at the window with all these great puzzles and adventures buzzing in my nut and, at the same time, trying to keep my face in the Ramon Novarro set which I had been practising in front of the looking-glass till I got it fixed.

M'mother was wearing her blue serge costume and best lacing-up black shoes and the blue hat with pearl hat pins sticking out. Annie had on her light-blue coat and button boots and the wee hat with silk roses on it that sits on the top of her head like a peerie. As well as my cordy roys, I was very gallus in a new cap with six panels, a strap across the front with buttons on each end and a button on the top.

–Can I go out and see James McAteer at the corner afore I go, Mammy?
–How many times do I have to tell you not to say 'afore'?
–Before I go.
–No, you will not and you with your good clothes on as well. You'll dirty yourself all over again.
–But, mammy, I have to see him.
–And we'll be going to the boat, soon.
–It's nearly an hour before we go.
–If you don't mind your P's and Q's m'boy, I'm going to turn another pin in your nose.
–But mammy I promised. . . . Only a wee while.
–If you're not back here in five minutes, we'll leave you behind, so we will.

I was out the door and down the stairs before she could change her mind. As I went through the close, the McGraws looked at me as if I had two heads because I had my good clothes on and it not Sunday.

–Look at him, all dressed up wi' nowhere to go!
–Are you dressed up for your Hallowe'en?
–Are you away to Hamilton to buy a new bell?

I didn't say anything in case I got into a fight and got my clothes ruined and then there would be trouble. Jimmy was under the lamp outside the Church of the Nazarene. He had a new McEwan's beer bottle top stuck in his jersey for a badge.

–I haven't got very long, I've to get right back.
–I hear your auntie's got a shop?
–Aye, she's got a sweetie shop in Derry.
–Maybe you could bring me back some sweeties.
–I'll pinch some for the gang. I'll keep a bag and every time I can, I'll keep filling up the bag and bring it back to share among the gang.
–Right. That's your orders. You've to bring back these sweeties or the gang will put you on trial and hang you from this lamp-post.
–Right, chief.

He wasn't the real chief, the big chief. That was George

Hall and when he wasn't there, Jambus McDougal, both bigger boys who were nearly ready to leave school and already going round with newspapers in the morning. But James had been made chief for that week. He stared up at the top of the Church of the Nazarene and fiddled with the beer bottle top on his jersey. He wasn't saying anything.

–James, you said you were going to tell me something. You said . . .

–What about?

–Eh. . . . You know.

–I've got a lot of things to think about this week.

–Aye. . . . But you said . . .

–There's a gang meeting tomorrow night.

–You said before I went . . . you'd . . .

–Oh. Yes. . . . That's right.

His face began to get a bit red.

–I found out all right.

–Well, what is it?

–I'll tell you. But don't pass it on to anybody else. Especially the wee boys. They're not supposed to know yet. We're big and we can know.

–Right. I'll keep it a secret.

–You know we've all got teapots. That you pee with. And the lassies have got split biscuits. I've seen one.

–Have you?

–Yes. I saw Beanie McMullin's. She showed it to me. Well, when they want to have a wean, your father gets his teapot and pees into your mammy.

–Pees into her?

–Aye. Into your mammy's split biscuit.

–You shouldn't be saying things like that.

–Well, you asked me to tell you.

–I don't believe they do that at all. You're only codding me.

–God's honour, fusey knuckle and spit.

–My old man wouldn't do that.

–That's what they do. They all do it. That's where you

came from. You're made inside your mammy when the pees gets mixed and then you're born.

–M'mammy and daddy would never do anything like that. Them are dirty things. They don't do dirty things. You'll go to hell. I'm away.

–What's the password?

–Corrabeestie.

–Corrabeestie. Don't forget the sweeties, Patrick, if you don't want to get hanged.

–All right, James. Would you like a bar of chocolate for yourself?

–Yes. Fry's Cream.

–But I don't believe you about what you said.

–It's true. All the bigger boys know it.

–Did your father do it?

–He must've.

–I'm away. I'll see you when I come back.

–Aye.

–Corrabeestie.

–Corrabeestie.

Later that night we were making our way to the boat by the shortcut down to the harbour along by the wagons beside the iron ore boats. You had to watch and not trip over the railway tracks or one of the ship's hawsers or a capstan. John and m'daddy were carrying the cases.

–Will you be all right then, Dan?

–Sure, we'll be all right. John here will do the cooking. We'll get plenty of old smokeboard and plenty of good fresh herrings from old McCanse.

–If you keep away from that oul' Nicol's Bar on Saturday nights.

–I won't be bothering at all, at all. I might just have a couple of wee dumps now and again.

–The quare couple of wee dumps.

–That's all I'll have. And John here will have his tuppenny packet of Woodbines every Friday.

–Yes, and I can get into the Casino for Andy Kane is taking the tickets and he lets me in.

–And you be sure and get some ribs from the wee man with the barrow. You get them fine and cheap and they'll make a good feed for you on Sunday.

–Guthrie the butcher always gives me a marrowbone and I can make soup.

–That's right. Don't go hungry whatever you do. Look at Patrick, he looks as if he's seen a ghost. What's wrong with you, child? Did you go to the lavatory before you came out?

–Aye. I'm all right, mammy.

–You've been as white as a sheet since you went out to see James McAteer. It's that gang, I suppose. Up to no good again.

Then Annie had to chime in.

–Them and their corrabeesties.

I just gave her a look that said you wait till I get you by yourself. I didn't want to talk very much to anybody. I did feel a bit sick kind of inside myself but I was not going to let on. It must have been a story he was telling me. It must have been fibs. Or maybe he had got it wrong. Maybe the bigger boys had told him that to make a fool of him. I was trying to picture what he told me but I couldn't.

Then we were at the boat. It was dusk and getting darker. There were two lit-up signs, one saying SALOON and a smaller one STEERAGE and this was the one we were steering for. The cases were put down and we stood for a while near the wagons which were still unloadering, two wee steam cranes swinging backwards and forwards and puttering away like billy-o. The name on the stern of the ship said LAIRDSLOCH in big gold letters and a board above an office in Winton Pier railway station said BURNS AND LAIRD SHIPPING LINE in black capitals.

Humming and hawing and whispering and squavering then began between the old fella and m'mother and I got that feeling in my stomach that told me I was going to be shoved into something which would have me squirming and red faced.

–Here, Patrick, take you this case and go along with John

up the gangway and if the man asks for your ticket, tell him you're just taking the cases on board for a wumman, says you. Go down them stairs and wait for Annie and me in the Steerage.

That was it. The old fella ruffed my hair saying remember squareshoulders, John said come on to keep behind him and say what he said and then I was staggering up the gangway with the heavy case, sometimes stepping on and sometimes between the wooden bars that would nearly break your ankle, the sudden feeling halfway across of being suspended in Limbo between the world on the quay and the new one of the ship, the gold buttons of the Second Mate with eyes above, a hand going up to scratch behind his ear —down on to the wooden deck, the smell of tarry rope and old sea water and stewed tea—lamps lighting the way along soupy passageways—down another dark stairway to a sour smell of bilge and cows' dung and cattle pens.

After a place was found on a wooden bench and cases left stacked there to stake a claim to it, we all stood at the deck rail searching for them finding m'daddy's pipe glowing under his cap among the wagons with the shorter figure of John beside him and you could look away over the tops of the wagons and the pug that would haul them away and it looked like a meccano model of a harbour and trains.

And then the model began to slip away from us and angle and become smaller, the two lonely sad figures on the quay, you could pick them up in your fingers and put them back in the box—tears running down m'mother's face and gleaming in the ship's lamps, her wounded hankie brought down fluttering—dying.

2

Away by myself at a place beside the rigging, I gazed out into the blackness of the horizon and laughed into myself at being free from school now for all of the Summer holidays and thought of Miss McPoldy—'Baldyanna'—with her frozen look and horn-rimmed specs.

Baldyanna is a noun,
Parse her up and parse her down,
Neuter gender, hopeless case,
Subject to her crabbit face.

The big black strap with the thongs on the end lying on her desk top where none of us could miss seeing it, she had lifted her long wooden pointer and, it being the end of term, the exams over, cracked her enamel, showing a gold tooth and said

–Because Patrick O'Connor got the highest mark for composition in the examination, he can come out and read to the class from this book here, as we are breaking up for the Summer holidays. I am sure you will all like that, children.

Mostly giggles from the girls, grunts from the boys and a raspberry from Eesky Dan, 'The worst boy in Saint Mary's Elementary School' which Miss McPoldy let pass.

–Read out the title, boy, and the pieces till I stop you.

I went out to the front, took the book from her and faced the class, Miss McPoldy behind me at her desk. I thought to myself she was probably reading *True Romances* or even *Comic Cuts* under the register. I opened the book.

–*Letters, Sentences and Maxims* by Lord Chesterfield. Groans from the class.

–YOUTHFUL EMULATIONS. 'This is the last letter I shall write to you as a little boy; for tomorrow, if I am not mistaken you will attain your ninth year; so that for the future I shall treat you as a *youth*. You must now commence a different course of life, a different course of studies. No more levity; childish toys and playthings must be thrown aside, and your mind directed to serious objects. . . .'

The thought came into my head that Miss McPoldy, sitting as she was behind me, although she could hear my voice, could not see my face and at this point I made the most lopsided, comical, pantomime face I could think of. A titter ran through the class. I restored my face to normal again.

–GOOD BREEDING. 'Though I need not tell one of your age, experience and knowledge of the world, how necessary good breeding is, to recommend one to mankind; yet as your various occupations of Greek and cricket, Latin and pitchfarthing, may possibly divert your attention from this object, I take the liberty of reminding you of it, and desiring you to be very well bred at Lord Orrery's. . . .'

Raspberry from Eesky Dan which brought the pointer rattling on the desk.

–Huggins!

–TRUE DECENCY. 'One of the most important points of life is decency; which is to do what is proper, and where it is proper; for many things are proper at one time and in one place, that are extremely improper in another. It is very proper and decent to dance well, but then you must dance only at balls and places of entertainment; for you would be reckoned a fool if you were to dance at a church or a funeral. . . .'

I made the daftest face I could think of and was rewarded by a laugh from the class. I suppose Miss McPoldy thought they were appreciating the wit of Lord Chesterfield.

–HOW TO DRESS. 'Take great care always to be dressed like the reasonable people of your own age, in the place where you are; whose dress is never spoken of one way or another, as either too negligent or too much studied.'

I stuck my tongue out as far as it would go and crossed

my eyes till they were looking at each other. The girls screamed and the boys collapsed. As the pointer banged on the desk I quickly returned to normal and the class stopped but there was now a buzz of held-in laughter.

–VULGAR PLEASURES. 'Many young people adopt pleasures for which they have not the least taste, only because they are called by that name. Gaming, that draws you into a thousand scrapes, leaves you penniless, and gives you the air of an outrageous madman, is another exquisite pleasure is it not?'

Here, I made a mad face.

–'As to running after women, the consequences of that vice are only the loss of one's nose, the total destruction of health and, not infrequently, the being run through the body.'

This with the popping eyes of someone who has just had a sword in his guts brought the house down. Miss McPoldy, sounding puzzled, allowed the class a good laugh before stopping them.

–MIMICRY. 'Mimicry, which is the common and favourite amusement of little, low minds, is in the utmost contempt with the great ones. It is the lowest and most illiberal of all buffoonery. . . .'

I mimicked Miss McPoldy and the girls were falling about in their seats. Eesky Dan was in stitches.

–COARSE AND VULGAR PLEASURES. 'Does good company care to have a man reeling drunk among them? Or to see another tearing his hair and blaspheming. . . ?'

–HOW 'TO WEAR' LEARNING. 'Wear your learning like your watch, in a private pocket; and do not pull it out and stroke it, merely to show that you have one. . . .'

Seeing my face to this one the class collapsed in uproar. When Miss McPoldy had quietened them and started me off again, she began to tell them off for laughing at what they were not supposed to. Then a lassie who was always sooking up to the teacher said that it wasn't the book it was Patrick O'Connor. Miss McPoldy then said they were not to laugh at me for I was only doing my best. But they couldn't stop even if they tried. I only had to twitch my nose or raise an eyebrow. Then Miss McPoldy began to catch on and finally she sneaked up behind and caught me suddenly doing Lon Chaney in THE HUNCHBACK OF NOTRE DAME. I got three with hands crossed and led back to my seat by the ear.

–. . . and you're the clown of the class, boy, the clown of the class!

That made me feel it was worthwhile for one of the things I wanted to be when I grew up was a clown. The others were a safe breaker like the Black Sapper, a film star like Ramon Novarro, a boxer like Gene Tunney, a footballer like Patsy Gallaher, a bushranger like Ned Kelly, an outlaw like Jesse James, a Freedom Fighter like Padraic Pearse and a tram-driver.

But the next day was the breaking-up day for the summer holidays and all you did was come in dressed in a good jersey and your Confirmation tie maybe—all the lassies in good pinnies with their hair in plaits—and sit in your places with books for what was called 'private reading', waiting for the time to march into the big hall. Private reading books were not *The Startler* or *Adventure, Wizard, Boy's Magazine*. Or *The Magnet* or *Gem*. Or American magazines like *Black Mask* or *Ace*. Some hopes. They weren't even *The Bullseye*. They were books that would send you to sleep like *Ivanhoe* or *Hereward the Wake* or books that would make you spew like *Little Women*.

Two big classrooms, Miss Mellon's and Miss McKay's, had been put together by taking down the partitions and later we all marched in here and sat around three sides looking at each other. I tried to get beside Barbara Reid to see if I could get my arm around her but Dan McGoogan beat me to it and I got shoved beside Lizzie Clark from Quay Street who always has snotters running from her nose. But you could have good fun tickling the girls on the seat in front and nipping the bums of the boys.

Then we had the presentation of the prizes by the Headmaster, Mister Scullion. Pat Tracy got the Dux Medal for that year—the highest prize in the world—and I got an old certificate of merit but not for attendance because I had plunked school a few times and two books, mouldy ones you could bet your parish boots—Poetry by Alfred Noyes and *The Life of Blessed John Bosco*. Miss Mellon's class sang *Golden Slumbers Kiss Your Eyes*. The bigger boys of the Advanced Division sang *The Raging Sea Did Roar* and, at the end, a boy came in pulling a long rope that seemed to have no end. He seemed to have a terrible job to pull this rope and went right out the door while the rope was still coming in. When it came to the end there was what was supposed to be a big boat but it was only a tanner boat from Woolworths and Mister Scullion had to look around sternly through his rimless spectacles as titters rose on all sides. Then we did our piece.

Eight boys in the class, including me, had to be a band and we came marching in singing

> *–Left, right, left, right, singing as we go,*
> *Left, right, left, right, marching in a row.*

We formed a half-circle and continued.

> *–We have Tommy boy for captain,*
> *Charlie he shall beat the drum—*

At this I stepped forward and beat the drum that was hanging round my neck on a string.

> *–Johnny boy for sergeant-major,*
> *You should wait to see us come—*

And then we all marched off singing

> *–Left, right, left, right, singing as we go,*
> *Left, right, left, right, marching in a row.*

After all the different classes had done their pieces, Mister Scullion got up and made a speech, telling us all to have a good holiday and come back ready to do greater things and, looking at Father Thornton, the Parish Priest, who was sitting beside him, he put in a bit about remembering to attend to our holy duties. Then, after Father Thornton had given us a blessing, the whole school rose and sang

–Mother of all that is pure and bright,
All that is bright and blest,
As we have taken our toils to thee,
So we will take our rest!
Take thou and bless our holiday,
All cows and horses stray lay-teet-see-ay!

3

The tanner boat pulled along on a rope was our boat now being pulled through the waves on a rope by the Red Hand of Ulster as he paddled through the Irish Sea to the Belfast Lough and staggered up the Cave Hill, the blood from his severed hand making the rope red.

Holding on to the rail I leaned back until I was looking up at the mast light probing a slowly swaying finger among the stars I saw up there. I brought my eyes down again to horizon level but left myself up there miles up looking down at the tanner boat as it began to heave and battle its way through the waves, its red and black funnel bravely steaming. I remembered the big puddle around our spicket in the backyard and me and Letty Taylor and Robert Cook and James McAteer sailing our boats, the Glen Sannox, the Juno, the Atlanta, the Belfast Boat and now here I was on it. Would somebody turn on a big spicket and make a storm?

I felt the rail beginning to strain against my hands and the sea crept further up the side of the ship and came nearer to me then dropped again and I felt myself lifted up as if on a swing. I turned and leaned against the rigging for support and there was m'mother's pale face half-way up this companionway and her voice calling me to come on down below it was getting rough as I felt on my face the spray from the first wave that had come over the ship's bows.

Below in the steerage I walked across the wooden deck trying to balance as it moved away from my feet and not slip where people had already been sick. Annie was stretched out on the bench with a coat over her. She was moaning and her face had turned a green colour against her red hair.

All around, you could hear these moans and weans crying and the cows in the pens were beginning to low and toss their heads and you could hear their hooves stamping and slithering on the deck as they tried to keep their feet. The smell of their dung was everywhere. For them, I suppose, the ground had never moved under their hooves before and I felt sorry for them and wanted to pat them. There were ropes along the deck to hang on to and along one of these came struggling a cattle man with a big stick in his hand and he went into the pens and began to croon and talk to the cattle and some of them looked at him with their big eyes as a wean looks at its mammy. The sea was beginning to come over the gunwale and nearly come up to our feet and then m'mother and I had to hold on to each other to keep from falling off the wooden bench which had handles all round it as the ship shuddered along its stem and pitched over like the steamboats at the fair and suddenly I saw us all in the sea holding on to these handles and trying to pull ourselves up on to the floating benches which were rafts. But a steward came down carrying a big tray with mugs of steaming tea. M'mother bought one and I had a drink and Annie sat up and managed to sip some. A while after I had the tea I began to feel sick. I reached the side of the ship and, holding on to the rope, got to where some air was coming in and you could see the sea going up and down. I held on to the rope and looked down at the water running out through the scuppers and over my boots, soaking my feet, and I couldn't do anything about it. I was lost. Alone. Cold sweat on me. In purgatory.

YOUR DADDY PEES INTO YOUR MAMMY.

I leaned over. My stomach heaved with the ship. Let this dirty sacrilege pass from me. Thankfully, I watched my spew mixing with the sea water and running out the scuppers.

Calm. While dreaming. Before waking. A smooth, lulling rhythm. Drowsily open lids, my mother's chiselled profile near. Her green eyes looking away. A wisp of hair blows on her brow. Her proud cheekbones etch a picture I saw sometime somewhere an Irish beauty on an old book of Celtic songs. I love her. I love her more than anything in the world. I want her warmth always near me her milk-smell always around me. She turns and her eyes smile to me. She puts out her hand to stroke my brow. My wee son, she says, making the world kind of whole.

I sat up and looked around me. It was daylight. Annie was already sitting up and managed to laugh as she looked at me. Her face was pale but not green anymore. The sour, bitter taste in my mouth reminded me I had been sick. But the deck was now only swaying gently. There was a tinge of blue in the sky.

–You slept well, son. Right through the storm. We're in the Belfast Lough.

–Did you sleep, Annie?

–I don't know. I must've. I woke up a wee while ago.

–Yes, Annie slept too, so she did, thanks be to God.

I stood up on the deck.

–I want a drink of water, mammy, my mouth's got a terrible taste in it.

–Aye, so it would, son. And you're the big enough boy to go up on the top deck and get a drink from the pump up there. And I'll give you a flannel and you can wash your face as well.

–Of course. That's nothing.

Out into the brightness of the early morning and looking up seeing heads over the rail on the saloon deck and above that the gold braid on the captain's cap looking out from the bridge, I climbed the companionway and turned down a passageway leading to the drinking well. Over on the starboard side blue green hills coming out of the mist, a tall lighthouse and the small white houses of a town. Looking over the side, the sea swishing past the ship was now a dark green. I rinsed my mouth out at the pump, had a drink and washed my face.

Soon, the water began to change to brown and then

become muddier as the lough narrowed. Then we were sailing past huge gantries—HARLAND AND WOLFFS—with half-built ships rusting on the slips and ocean liners moored alongside, the size of which up till now I had only seen on cigarette cards—rows and rows of bunkers piled high with coal—tall chimleys—entrances to smaller harbours running off the main docks with glimpses of tramp ships with foreign flags the same as you would see in Ardrossan—more big ships moored along the quay—then the telegraph rang and we stopped engines. People were crowding around an iron gate in the ship's side but I could see over their heads ropes tightening and jerking as the ship began to swing round then a bridge came into view with people looking at us and tram-cars passing behind them. Two sailors opened the iron gates and stood by them then we were tying up against the dock and a gangway was being lowered into place.

An officer was taking tickets at the gangway and when it was our turn to go past him I felt a push in my back and staggered down on to the dock with a case. When I looked back m'mother was talking away ten to the dozen to the officer and smiling away to him—'he's only a child, so he is'—holding up all the rest of the people trying to get off. Annie was squavering about with a red face even though she had a half-ticket then finally with the pressure from the people and the cajoling the officer waved them past and we were all on the dockside together.

The new smell of a strange land and the funny feeling that the cobbles are moving under your feet after the rolling and heaving of the ship.

Barrows clanging and clattering over the cobbles in a wooden shed the size of a parish hall and the smell of Indian corn in bags and scattered underfoot, the pigeons making a beanfeast, and men with leather belts with hooks stuck in them and big long moustaches like m'daddy's.

I would make this the subject of another composition at school and maybe win another silver threepenny bit from Mister Scullion as I did regularly nearly every month. I would maybe write a story about it in the jotter book full of stories which I carried about with me.

We moved across a cobbled square with a big clock tower in the middle and Irish jaunting cars around it and found a working men's eating house where we had pork sausages and Belfast baps, sitting among the dockers and shipyard workers and a few sailors all of them talking away with m'daddy's twang. But they lowered their voices when m'mother went up to the counter to get the tea and one of them was told to mind his language there was a lady present and they were all round her helping and carrying things for her and making Annie blush and patting me on the head. In the end I got fourpence in pennies and Annie got a threepenny bit.

Then with a laughing chorus of ta-ta's behind us we were away again carrying the cases along Dock Street and around a corner, having to stop and rest every so often because the cases were heavy and when m'mother bent over me I could see that her forehead was damp and a wisp of hair had come down again and I tried not to think of the other thing.

All the time m'mother was talking away about the streets and sights around us.

– . . . and here look, York Street and oh, there's the Burlington with the sausages frying in the window—d'ye not mind your father telling you about that eating house?—And look Royal Avenue, ah dear, ah dear, d'y'see the City Hall there? Aye, the City Hall, your father helped to build that, so he did, ha-ha, yes, he worked at the building of that for a while, when there was work to be got—and look North Queen Street, d'ye see this big church here and the bullet marks in the stones, Tt-Tt-Tt, yis the bullet marks in the stones, that's from the time of the royits so it is, when the armoured cars were going about oul' Belfast, God help us, and there was a curfew on and your father was nearly shot dead more then once so he was—I was in the terror of my life most of the time and him in the Sarsfield

Guards and all, they were looking for him, so they were, isn't that why he had to go to Scotland—Look, see down there, d'y'see down there, that's Paddy's Market in Smithfield, I wish I had the time to go down there, many's the bargain I got down there—And look, we cut up this road here, see the man selling the corn cure on that stall over there?—That would take all the corns off your feet, aye and mind you I could do with some of that at this minute, so I could for my feet are nearly dropping off me, so they are—Look, there's the Al'ambra over there, yis, the Al'ambra, I'm sure many's the time you've heard your father speaking about the Al'ambra, look, would you believe it, it's got pictures in it now, they're showing pictures now, there's no more variety—pictures it is, whose this? Tim McCoy, one of them oul' cowboys—and here we are, aye and not a minute before time, says you—H.M.S. Catherwood's buses, oh and look, oh would you believe it there's one going to Dublin, all the way to Dublin now—your granny used to live there in Rathmines, so she did—that's your father's mother—yes, she lived in Dublin for a long time, so she did—Glory be to God, all the way to Dublin—There's one going to Coleraine—and here, here's the Derry bus, our bus is in, so it is, the bus is in, run you on Patrick and get on before it goes away without us—and go you up right up to the back and keep down and out of sight where nobody will see or hear you.

It was a good job I was wee for my age, even though I was getting on for eleven and could coorie down on the back seat but still I got fed up always being called a child. But this conductor wasn't bothering anyway. The bus stuck away out over the back wheels and I was rattled up and down like a pea in a whistle all the way to Derry.

Then we got off the bus and struggled along with the cases again up a street called Shipquay Street, around a square called the Diamond into Ferryquay Street. This was a busy street with a lot of motors and carts and horses and sometimes a pony and trap. M'mother stopped outside a shop with big windows and a tiled entrance, above which it said HIGH CLASS CONFECTIONERS.

As we followed her inside a smell of chocolate met us and Annie turned and looked at me, her eyes glistening as we saw big glass cases with doors on them full of chocolate boxes going right up to the ceiling and bottles and bottles of sweets, it was like going into a dream. Then a tall straight-backed lady with a black velvet band round her throat came from behind the counter and kissed m'mother and ushered us all into a back room where Bridget rushed towards us with her arms open.

4

Bridget, who I remember seeing only when she came home for a week-end from the big houses where she used to work and once when she had visited me in hospital, was now as big as, in fact bigger than m'mother. She had dark frizzy hair, a string of pearls around her neck, a handbag and that powder on her face. She had laughing, crinkly eyes, was nearly always in a good temper, spoke very proper and knew how to serve the customers in the shop. A real big girl she was. She would give me a penny or twopence now and again to buy a *Rover* or a *Startler*.

On my first day there I got out as soon as I could and began to explore around. Right opposite there was a Woolworths—nothing over sixpence—and I went in here with Annie and walked around all the counters but she always wanted to look at girl's things, hankies and dolls and perfume and that and not at the trains or the playing cards. When I got the chance I went away by myself down to the Diamond and had a look at the statues of soldiers with fixed bayonets and went right round where there were flowers and people sitting on seats, and looked on the ground to see if I could find anything. I discovered a picture house called the RIALTO and had a look at the billboards and the photos outside. Oh boy! They were showing a picture called *Romance* all that week with Ramon Novarro who I am trying to look like and next week *The Yellow Mask* with Lupino Lane, so I must get m'mother to take me or maybe Bridget would when she gets a night off or maybe I could get to a matinee by myself. Then I found a lane off Shipquay Street where men in bowler hats were going in and out of a big bank and I hung about here for a long while asking had they any cigarette cards please and collected quite a few before dinner time which was great, stewing meat with lovely gravy and new potatoes and turnips, different from back home.

That evening it was very busy in the shop with very well-dressed people coming in and out and Aunt Annie was bowing and smiling away and talking pan loaf ten to the dozen and all the time Bridget's high-pitched voice could be heard talking proper and laughing away. M'mother was helping by bringing out cartons of sweets and opening them up whenever they were required. I heard her saying that there was a big function on in the Guildhall and that's where all the swells were going with the high-class chocolates like *Barker Dobsons* or *Terry's* or *Chanticleer* liqueurs.

Whenever I could, I slipped into the shop and got behind the counter and it was a great thrill to be on the other side for the first time then Bridget chased me away saying she was too busy but Aunt Annie slipped some caramels into my hand as I was going.

As they were all busy with the shop and even Annie was helping m'mother, I went from the back room into a long, narrow passageway behind. This is where the trap-door was that led down to the cellar where all the stock was kept in big cartons and cases. I stepped over it carefully in case somebody would pull a lever somewhere like Sweeney Todd the barbers and you would be pitched headlong down the stairs. Just past this was a window that you couldn't see through because the panes were frosted glass but there was a corner underneath where you could be by yourself.

I stood looking at the window but not seeing the window and began to imagine pictures in my mind. I would let the pictures run until I stopped the reel at one. Then I would clench my fists and squeeze myself and work up a feeling till I was in the picture and everything else would fade away and it would be as if I could climb out of my skin and be something else whenever I wanted to be. I clenched my fists and squeezed and hopped from foot to foot till there was the Belfast Boat rushing through the waves at a hundred knots—I the captain in full dress uniform drive it from the bridge not with a ship's wheel but a steering wheel like a racing motor's—the buoys in the lough whizzing past like telegraph poles up to the landing stage reversing engines and stopping dead right on the exact spot where the ship should be—crowds cheering from the bridge flags and bunting everywhere. I take off my helmet with goggles and wave them to the crowd—then on to my horse in one jump and gallop away over the mountains into the desert—after three days there is no more water and I am slowly dying of thirst clawing at my throat but my horse dies first—I have to shoot him to put him out of his agony and I stagger on my boots wearing down until when I am almost dead from thirst and can't go on much longer there is this township but the street seems to be deserted—then a little building of corrugated iron. I hear voices coming from it singing hymns and this is a church and I stagger in and down the aisle as everybody turns and stares at this bearded stranger but I manage to get right down to the altar and the priest turns round and raises his hand and blesses me and I lay the child on the altar steps and say to the priest do you forgive me father and he says I forgive you sure you didn't know what you were doing.

I had to stop because tears were coming into my eyes so I came back into myself again. I hummed and hawed and daddledeeda'd for a while to get used to where I was then I went back into the other room and sat on the bed with my jotter writing down things I had seen that day for compositions and looking at big words in my pocket dictionary that John had got from an old bookstall for going for a message and given to me.

Later that night after the shop was closed we all sat around in the back. Bridget made porridge and we had that with buttermilk, m'mother saying it made you sleep well so it did. There was an old blanket across the door to keep the light from shining out into the shop and Aunt Annie said to us now we must all be very quiet. It was a lock-up shop and nobody was supposed to be living in it at all and we were all breaking the law and the fire regulations. Later we heard heavy footsteps coming along the pavement and into the shop's entrance and auntie said now not a sound, not a peep out of you. I held my breath and looked at Annie and her eyes were popping and the ferntickles were standing out on her face against the white but I nearly made her laugh so she had to look away quickly and m'mother gave her a dunt and said to wheesht you gerl. My auntie whispered not to breathe a sound it was the police and we heard the lock rattling as it was tried then the footsteps going away and we all let out a sigh of relief.

I was to share a narrow bed with Annie, her at the top and me at the bottom, m'mother and Bridget in another one and auntie in a camp bed which she had rigged up. But before we went to bed auntie made us all get down on our knees and say the Rosary, the five joyful mysteries—one a night—and I got the chance to make Annie laugh again but she had to keep it in and I had her nearly bursting but when I looked up Aunt Annie was looking at me with a slight frown but her eyes were laughing and she seemed to be echoing m'daddy and saying into herself Patrick you're a villain.

5

–For often in O'Connor's van
To triumph dashed each Connaught clan . . .
. . . Sing, oh! They died their land to save
At Aughrim's slopes and Shannon's wave . . .

. . . But hark! a voice like thunder spake
The West's awake! The West's awake!
Sing, oh! Hurrah! Let England quake,
We'll watch till death for Erin's sake!

I was washing myself at the sink down the passageway and I remembered m'father and mother talking between them and saying did you never hear Annie in Derry sing *The West's Awake* and now here she was singing it while frying sausages for the breakfast on the stove not far from the sink.

–The chainless wave and lovely land
Freedom and nationhood demand! . . .

I wondered what O'Connor's van was, if we had anything to do with it and if it was the same van that figured in another song m'daddy used to sing *The Smashing of the Van.* There was something different and sad and mysterious about these songs, they were not the same as other songs, the singers always had a glint of defiance in their eye. There was a great wrong that had to be righted. A dark beauty held captive by the Black and Tans. When I grew up and left school I would ask the old fella if he could get me into the Sarsfield Guards. I would put on my jacket green and knee breeches and a hat with a buckle on the front and not rest till I had freed the dark beauty from bondage.

And now I watched my aunt as she stood straight-backed and sung out loud and proudly. M'mother said she would wake the nuns over in the convent and they all had a laugh.

Then we sat down to our breakfast and m'mother said these were lovely Irish pork links, you didn't get them like that across the water and the good soda farls it was lovely so it was.

My auntie went visiting once a week and I was being taken with her this time while Bridget and m'mother looked after the shop. I was dressed in my best clothes, a white shirt with my Confirmation tie and brown boots. My left foot was hurting a bit owing to a bone which stuck out in the wrong place since I fell down the Bath Rocks. All new boots and shoes hurt my foot until the bone had worn its own groove into the leather and this took a long time but I was used to it. Soon we were ready to leave and m'mother whispered to me to be sure and behave myself and not disgrace her in front of the swells.

Ferryquay Street had a fresh smell as we came out into it, the carts had been round spraying and the sun was shining and reflecting on the brass plates and lettering of the big bank on the other side. My auntie was dressed like a lady in the pictures with a hat and a veil over her eyes and a fur round her shoulders and as she walked along holding me by the hand she received respectful nods and words on all sides. Good morning, Miss O'Connor—Nice morning, Miss O'Connor. Gentlemen raising their hats and some stopping to speak. A fine day, Miss O'Connor and who is the little man?—This is my wee nephew from across the water—A nice wee fella he is too—A threepenny piece slipped into my hand. A good day to you, Miss O'Connor—A fine day it is, surely—A lovely day, God be praised.

We turned into The Diamond and then into Longtower Street, the name lifting my mind again to green country and whitewashed cottages, the towers and Celtic crosses behind them and there was the bus that would be going there coming towards us, a secret looking bus with a wee dark man in a peaked cap peering from behind a big round wooden steering wheel and LIMAVADY in faded letters on the front. That must be the place. There is where your dreams would come true. Where the crock of gold would be—LIMAVADY. But auntie stopped another bus, a corporation bus. When we got off she said this is WATERSIDE.

I felt very wasted after walking with my aunt up a path, through a garden and ringing a bell and a maid had led us into a big room with polished tables and book-cases like McKellar's sale-room back home and thick carpets on the floor and flowers everywhere and chairs that looked like you would get into a row if you sat on them. All around the room sat swanky ladies, a good number of them in heliotrope costumes with coffee-coloured lace across their bosoms and if you had laid all the ropes of pearls on end they would have reached to Paddy's Milestone. A good number of them also had black velvet bands around their throats like my aunt and some were quizzing away like lighthouses through their gold-rimmed glasses. Then their voices began to come from every direction.

–Now Annie, that's a nice little lad you have with you. Is that your little nephew you've been telling us about?

–Yes. This is my little man.

–And what age is the wee lad?

–Oh, he's getting on for eleven, now.

–Is that right? Well, and I would never have believed it. Mind you, he's wee for his age.

–He's small but he's wiry.

–But hasn't he the nice little baby face?

–He has.

–Oh, he has.

–Hasn't he now?

–He's got a very sweet wee face, so he has.

–Ah, and look at him, he's shy, too. Are you shy, sonny? Are you a wee bit shy?

–Ah, he's shy, so he is.

–Are you shy then, son?

My tongue had cleaved to the roof of my mouth.

–Ah, he doesn't want to say anything, so he doesn't.

–Past ten. I would never have believed it. His wee, shy face.

–He's clever. He's a clever boy. His mother has been

telling me that he got the prize for English composition.

–Is that right? He's a clever wee man.

Prodding me. Bending down over me. Their lockets swinging in front of my eyes. Peering into my face.

–And he's tidy, too.

–He's a lovely, wee man, so he is.

–What is your name, then?

–Won't you tell us your name?

Auntie bent down and whispered in my ear. I realised that my fists were clenched tight by my sides, my hands sticky, the nails digging into the flesh. Hot faced, I looked up from under a shamed head. Eyes all round me. Fingers prodding me. Voices. They were going to strip me. They were going to lift my shirt up and look at me. They were going to examine my body. I was back on the operating table again.

–Be a good boy and don't let me down now, my little sonny man.

Auntie was whispering in my ear again. I made saliva come into my mouth and got my tongue unstuck. I made my mouth work.

–P . . . P—Patrick.

–Now, there's a fine name for you.

–Patrick, is it?

–Is he called after Ireland's holy patron saint?

–You couldn't get a better name than that.

–Hail, glorious Saint Patrick.

My mouth eased and my fists unclenched. I could lean on my crozier. I could look up at them all and pull my cloak around me. My cloak that was green and gold and encrusted with rubies and pearls. The snakes writhing around my feet. I had only to lift my right hand with the finger crooked and they would all get down on their knees in front of me.

–Oh, he's a clever boy, so he is. A bit of a comedian too, his mother was telling me. Doesn't he come home and imitate the whole cast when he goes to the pictures? Yes, the whole cast, don't you know? Lionel Barrymore.

He does Lionel Barrymore. And Victor McLaglen. And, oh, Eddie Cantor, he is very good at Eddie Cantor. Of course I never get to the pictures myself, I am much too busy with the business—meeting all the travellers, as well, aren't they always wanting me to give them an order for this, that and the other, oh, they would pester the life out of you—yes, he can imitate a fiddle as well. You wouldn't know the difference. Would you do something here for us now, Patrick? Would you do something for the good ladies of the Sodality?

–Oh, wouldn't that be splendid!

–Go on, the great little man!

–Ah, dear, ah, dear!

–What is this he's going to do? I didn't hear that.

–Oh, he's going to perform, so he is.

–Is that right?

–He is to go on the stage, so he is.

–Would you look at that.

Auntie Annie bent down, smiling at me again, looking very affectionate. She whispered in my ear again.

–Would you say 'A Pretty, Young Colleen named Kitty O'Toole'?

She helped me up on to a chair. I looked around the assembled crowd who had come from far and wide to receive my blessing. I looked at them from behind my beard with holy eyes.

–OCH, BOYS, HOW I ENVIED MCGINTY!

A pretty, young colleen was Kitty O'Toole,
The Lily of sweet Tipperary,
With a voice like a thrush,
And cheeks like a rose,
And a figure as nate as a fairy!

Sure, I've seen her meself in the good Summertime,
In the glory of sweet one and twinty,
As she sat with McGinty's big arm round her waist,
Och, boys, how I envied McGinty!

Well, it wasn't that long, 'bout a month, maybe more,
When meself and the boys were invited
By Mickey O'Toole from the cabin beyond
To see Kate and McGinty united.

And there in the church they were made into one,
And the priest gave them blessings in plinty,
And as I saw him kissed by the beautiful Kate,
Och, boys, how I envied McGinty!

Well, the time it did pass, poor McGinty, he died,
And my heart was nigh broken with pity
To see that young widow so lonesome and sad—
So I went and got married to Kitty!

But now as I look where McGinty is laid,
With a stone o'er his head cold and flinty,
And see him lie there, so peaceful and calm—
Och, boys, how I envy McGinty!

And then it was murder. They all wanted to kiss me and most of them did. Oh gads. Ee, gads.

Away in a corner by myself, I opened my jotter book to read what I had written down.

July 4. My Auntie Annie is next to Janet Gaynor. She smiles to me. She pats me on the head but it doesn't make me feel wasted because I like the feel of her hand. She is very kind. When I go out for a walk with Annie she never lets us go past the counter without stopping us and giving us a bag of sweets to take along. She always says you should sit up straight in the chair and she has got a very straight back. She has very good manners and speaks very proper but she is not stuck up. She wears a gold locket sometimes and a gold wristlet watch. She always calls Bridget BRIDIE. She is great.

July 7. PLACES ANNIE AND I HAVE BEEN WHEN WE GO FOR A WALK.

1. We went to the Walls of Derry. Up some steps then on to the walls and we went all the way round. Inside used

to be the town but now it is on both sides. We saw the big cannon called Roaring Meg. Annie said it was not as big as the one on the Castle Hill back home but I said it was bigger. We had a fight but I don't kick her with my boots anymore because I am bigger. All the way round are gates—Shipquay Gate, Ferryquay Gate—and they used to be the gates of the city. We came right back to where we started from. It was a great walk. When we told m'mother she made a terrible face saying Derry's Walls, oul' Derry's Walls and Roaring Meg, she would blow it up, so she would. 2. The Church of Saint Columcille. 3. The Rialto. Talkies. Outside ALL TALKING, SINGING, DANCING. We saw *Sunny Side Up* with Janet Gaynor, oh boy! I tried to imagine a kiss during the picture. Oh, what a thrill! Annie asked me if she was a bit like Janet Gaynor and I said she was plumb loco, baby. I asked her whose mummy was she. She said who did I mean. I said I knew, she was The Mysterious Mummy That Came To Life. 4. A walk down Longtower Street to Longtower Cathedral. We met some boys and lassies crossing a waste ground and we talked to them for a while. They called me a wee Scotty, a wee Scotty fella but they were all right. Some big boys asked Annie if she would like to come up behind the rock. If she came up they would give her a stalk of rock and brandy balls. Her face got red and she pulled me away. What was her face red for? 5. Waterside. We went right down Shipquay Street to the docks on the Foyle, down a stone stairway and on to a wee ferry. It was a motor boat and the man stood at the stern steering it with a rudder. That was great. We saw some big boats tied up and there was a Burns and Laird boat going to Glasgow and one to Dublin. Halfway across you could see right down to the end of the docks where Lough Foyle began and, if you looked the other way, up the river, it got narrower and narrower. As it was Saturday we went to the matinee in Waterside and saw *What Price Glory?* with Edmond Lowe and Victor McLaglen as Captain Flagg and Sergeant Quirt.

July 9. I like Aunt Annie nearly as much as m'mother

and father. Nearly as much as John. As much as Janet Gaynor. Better than Bridget. Annie doesn't count.

July 16. Last night after I went to bed I looked over the bedclothes and saw auntie in nothing but long, grey combinations in the light of a nightlight. She was combing and brushing her hair which falls right down to her waist. It is a light auburn colour and she wears it up in a bun during the day. I couldn't see very well but she had a glad neck and it was shining white in the dimness. Do aunties have a split biscuit as well? Would it be a different kind? I wish she would give me a kiss, X, X, X.

July 19. This would make a good story which I could write and send to *The Weekly News.* One day, while Aunt Annie was out on business, I was looking in the big boxes which were piled around the wall in the back room where we slept. I had coaxed m'mother to let me do this, promising not to touch anything and put everything back as I found it or auntie would give us all a row. Annie was also having a look now and again but she was in the nerves as usual. There were chocolate rabbits and hens and monkeys. There were chocolate angels. There were little chocolate dancers in ballet skirts. Chocolate Cinderellas. Chocolate babies descending on parachutes. Golden coaches pulled by chocolate horses. There were huge padded silk boxes almost as big as myself tied with coloured ribbons. There was every chocolate delight in the land of confectionery. Exploring further by climbing up to the shelves on a ladder, lo and behold, in a box I discovered a little Santa Claus, fully dressed with a sack of silver-paper-wrapped sweets on his back! But, wonder of wonders, when I had taken him out and brought him down the ladder, there was a key on his back to wind him up and when you put him on the floor, he walked! M'mother was Tt-Tt-Tting and saying watch yourself, child, but I was lost to the world with this great new toy when suddenly Bridget shouted in from the shop and m'mother said quick, auntie was just returning. Quickly, I shoved the toy under the bed out of sight as auntie came in, smiling and drawing off her gloves and me sitting there with my most innocent face. Tired, she sat down with a sigh and we were all sitting round looking at her, most of us stiff-faced, when out from underneath the bed, straight between her legs came walking the little Santa Claus! I didn't know where to look but auntie just smiled and patted my head and said had I been playing with her little man? Then we all just doubled up laughing.

July 20. There is a wee hole in the partition between the back room and the passageway where the sink is and the window where you can be by yourself and I could hear Bridget and m'mother talking. There she was, they were saying, getting up every morning to go to holy communion. Every morning, mind you. They were sure she was a saint. And she never missed the nuns coming round. And didn't they know where to come to? Always with their hands out, God forgive us. She was making the Nine Fridays and umpteen novenas to Saint Anthony. And down on her knees every night praying to the Sacred Heart. A saint. Ah, but m'mother thought she was a wee bit eccentric. She was a wee bit eccentric in her ways. Sure, all the O'Connors were a bit eccentric anyway, not like the Dooleys, her side of the family. Sure our Uncle Dan was eccentric as well. Our Uncle Dan in Cushendun that had so many sheep on the hill he couldn't count them. It was him that set Aunt Annie up in business. But he was eccentric as well. Didn't he leave our father an oul' fiddle when he died, an oul' fiddle. But sure, he never got the fiddle as it turned out, she didn't know who got it but he was swindled out of it, so he was. For the fiddle was stuffed with money, so it was. No, he never got it. Eccentric, the lot of them.

Why does she call Aunt Annie eccentric? What does she mean? Why were they talking about her behind her back? What was the mystery of the old fiddle? I am not great with them now for saying things about my auntie.

July 21. Oh boy, we're off to Buncrana tomorrow!

6

DOHERTY'S it said on the side of the green bus lined up with other buses in a street off Foyle Street. They were not like the A.1. Service buses back home but more like the old bus that Mick Kelly used to run or Cunningham's THE STAR— wee square BEANS sitting low on the road with windows bigger than the tin sides. I saw the LIMAVADY bus again, not the size of tuppence, but the wee dark man had disappeared. The Buncrana bus came in and the three of us got on through a folding door. Auntie was already down there for a few days seeing to the new shop which someone had been looking after and Bridget was left in Derry to look after the other shop with an assistant coming in during the day to help her. M'mother was to serve in the Buncrana shop and auntie would be up and down between the two. I was shoved up to the back as usual and squashed but the conductor was a jokey man who kept the whole bus laughing and he didn't ask anything for me. After we had been driving for a while out of Derry to the outskirts and into the country, m'mother said we would be coming to the border soon between Northern Ireland and the Irish Free State.

I saw what looked like a big barn in the distance and it got nearer and nearer until it looked as if we were going to drive into it and that is just what we did and it turned out to be the Customs Shed, the road went right through it and the border crossed it and there were platforms along both sides, one of which we drew up at.

The folding door opened and a Customs Officer with a waxed moustache stood on the steps, looked around the bus with glittering eyes and shouted

–Anything liable for duty!

Everybody sat very still in their seats and said not a word.

He put his hand up and twirled the ends of his moustache till they looked like spikes sticking up.

–Anything liable for duty?

You couldn't hear a pin drop.

He came into the bus and began to move down the centre, prodding parcels and asking what was in them and examining goods in the luggage racks. He stopped at a big fat woman three seats in front of us who had a large brown paper parcel under her seat. He prodded the parcel with his foot.

–What's in this parcel?

–Ah, it's nothing, nothing at all.

–What is in this parcel?

–Ah sure, I wouldn't be bothering with that at all, it's nothing, nothing at all.

–What is it?

–It wouldn't be any good to the likes of you, sir.

–What?

–You wouldn't want this, mister honey.

–Is—

–You wouldn't have any use for this at all, your worship.

–Would you—

–Fine big strong fella that you are. You'd be destroyed before you would want the likes of this.

–Would you be telling me what's in the parcel itself?

–And wasn't I only after buying it in Woolworths and it didn't cost me hardly a make, so it didn't.

–And, and—

–Away you along, son, it's not the like of me you would want to be bothering.

–What is—

–And you a chief as well. . . .

The woman's face was getting redder and redder and the ends of the officer's moustache were standing up straighter and straighter.

–Yerrah, I'm sure you would be up for promotion soon, captain, the way you wouldn't want to be chastising the likes of a widow woman and her with three bits of childher to bring up in a hard world.

The officer bent down, fished the parcel from under the seat and placed it in the woman's lap with everybody in the bus, including the driver and conductor, looking on with their mouths open.

–I'll thank you, madame, to open this parcel at once.

–Ah, sure you're only codding me. I know you've a grand way with the ladies, so you have.

–Otherwise, the property will be seized.

The woman leaned forward in her seat and touched a man in front on the shoulder.

–Would you give us the hoult of that knife you're snedding your tobacco with, mister.

–Gladly, daughter, gladly.

The officer drew back but the woman wanted only to cut the string of the parcel quickly. This she did, drawing the contents out and sticking it under the officer's nose—a great big porcelain chanty-po, twice as big as the one we keep under the bed at home.

–There y'are now, d'ye see that? How much duty d'ye want for that? Would you like to do your duty on that?

The Customs Officer retreated hastily saying

–Get this bus on at once!

And the whole bus collapsed in an uproar of shouting and laughing. People came from the front to pat the woman on the back. The bus drove away but it was some time before the driver could keep it on a straight course, he was laughing so much and a man who had been drinking from a bottle began to sing

–Murphy sat on the top of the cart
Houlding the crock on his knee!

And everybody was laughing and singing and men drinking out of bottles and one man stood up and took off his jacket and there was another jacket underneath and he took this off as well and there was another one under that and when he had climbed out of two pairs of trousers there were two waistcoats draped around his haunches to make two new suits. Then the fat woman stood up, taking off her costume jacket, and miraculously began to shed weight, peeling off silk stockings and other new clothes from all around her. It was like this all over the bus and the driver and conductor couldn't stop laughing. Then Annie started till the tears ran down her face and m'mother had a pain in her side and I was helpless and the man at the front singing away.

–Oh, won't you buy my neck-a-tie,
My collar and my stud?
Oh, they call me hokey-pokey
But my goods they are the best,
Oh, won't you buy off the nice-a sheeny-man!

And it was like this, laughing and singing, the bus fairly bursting at the seams, all the way into Buncrana, Donegal.

7

And there, as the bus stopped outside the barracks of the Gardai and we got off, across on the other side by the fork of a road, was THE LOUGH SWILLY FRUITERERS AND CONFECTIONERS with Aunt Annie standing outside, smiling a welcome to us. She took us straight through the shop—smell of tomatoes packed in straw, oranges and chocolate—into a kitchen at the back which was itself the size of our attic back home. Here, we sat at a big, square, scrubbed table facing a range which took up nearly all the space of one wall at which a woman was baking scones on a griddle and making tea. Auntie introduced her to us as Cassie who came in to help her during the day. And we had these lovely home-baked scones from the griddle and mugs of strong tea. Afterwards, Cassie helped us upstairs with the cases to the third floor where our room was. There was a big bed and a small bed in a corner under a window. Annie was to go with m'mother into the big bed.

I could hardly believe it. For the first time in my life I had a bed to myself.

The cookalookalooing of a cock woke me in the morning. The others had gone from the room and I lay by myself looking at the tops of trees through the window and a rainpipe with a nest in it and a bird darting out and in and whistling. It was sunny and the window was open a bit and through it came the scent of hay and flowers and smells of cooking from downstairs. I could hear the faint hum of voices from the kitchen.

A door opened, bringing the buzz up louder and Aunt Annie's voice called up the stairs to her little man, Patrick, to come down as his breakfast was ready. I dressed quickly and went down into the kitchen and sat at the big table and ate a boiled, new-laid, brown egg with soda farls and wheaten scones and Irish creamery butter and watched Cassie working at the range baking scones on a griddle and stirring pots while m'mother and auntie bustled in and out of the shop, a wee bell tinkling above the door. Cassie told me that Annie had been sent up to the Italian shop to get five hundred Player's cigarettes wholesale.

The kitchen led into a large scullery with a window looking on to a backyard. I went through and opened a door and stepped out on to the dirt surface. Behind the scullery a shed with an old two-wheeled barrow rusting away. A fence separating our yard from Doherty's next door. Here, a goat was tethered. It looked up at me with sad eyes and bleated. At the bottom of the yard a hedge with a field beyond, two horses in the far corner. I watched them move about the field. They came nearer to where I was then one came right up and put its head over the hedge. It looked at me. I was a bit scared to go too near but I went up until I could see breath coming from its nostrils and a fly on its head between the lugs. Then it tossed its mane suddenly, turned and galloped away back to the other horse. I went into the shed and stood beside the old barrow to be by myself. There were two big horse-shoes nailed up on the wall and a hatchet and a cleaver in a corner. They were all rusty. Doherty's goat bleated again. I felt sad.

It was a good sunny day and I liked my breakfast and Cassie, and I wanted to try and get a kiss from Aunt Annie and this was a great shed, it could be my own gang-hut and then there were the horses in the field that I could maybe get a saddle on and ride away to free Ireland. And there was the goat.

But then there was what James McAteer had told me as well. You couldn't get away from it.

My mother in her clean white blouse and blue serge skirt. Grey stockings going up under. They were tucked under her knickers at the knee, the elastic held her stockings up. I had seen her in her knickers when I was a wean. Long light-grey drawers down to the knee. I sat on her lap and fondled her tits. She opened her blouse. I took one of them in my hands and held it. The skin was smooth and silky. There was a rosebud on the end which was swelling and ripe. She looked down at me over her white bosom, her mouth open, her breath sweet. She kissed me. I put the rosebud in my mouth and sucked the cream. I looked into her eyes and sucked and kneaded to a rhythm rocking on her lap. Her eyes looking deeper into mine, she touched her lips with her tongue.

Tell it, g'on, tell it. No. Yes, once I saw her taking down her knickers and her creamy bum was bare naked before she disappeared behind the head of the big bed and I could hear her peeing into the po.

These are bad thoughts, you should put them out of your head—but they keep coming in again.

Oh, my God, I am very sorry that I have sinned against thee, because thou art so good, and I will not sin again. Amen.

M'daddy in his blue serge Sunday suit with his good cap and black boots laced and polished. I stood outside a pub in Countess Street waiting for him to come out. He has gone in to get another wee dump as he calls it before the bus comes because it is Saturday and he has had a winner. He gives me another penny to put in my pocket as he comes out and takes me by the hand.

–Come on and we'll have a pumpship. We must have an oul' pumpship.

I thought he said a pump shit at first, he was swearing, and I felt rotten for m'daddy never says dirty words. But then he said it again, it was a *ship*. He meant a pee. He calls it a pumpship and when he said it to me I felt two feet taller, he was talking to me like a man. In the gentlemen's lavatory he unbuttoned my trouser flies and took out my teapot and held it while I peed. Then he stood where I had been standing and put his legs apart and straightened up and looked up at the sky and the sound of his pee was like a waterfall.

It splashed against the enamel and gurgled away down the hole. Then he bent his legs and although he tried to hide it from me I couldn't help seeing his tosshel before he stuffed it back into his trousers. It was different from mine, tan not pink, wrinkled but with a head like a serpent. Will I have to tell this in confession? I like m'daddy better than any man in the whole world.

Then how could he and m'mother. . . ? How could he do this to m'mother? Would it hurt her? It must hurt. My mother and father would not do dirty things. She is in the Sacred Heart Confraternity and goes to Communion every week and he never misses a month and sometimes twice a month if there is a special intention. Dirty things. Only the McGraws do dirty things and the heathens over in Herald Street and Kilmahew Street and Black Maggie and The Ghost who hang around the sailors in Nicol's Bar and Kee-Kee Tam opening his legs and showing his teapot to the two wee girls down the Bath Rocks. The men nearly killed him and left him for dead. What can I do?

Right behind the barrow into the corner where it smells musty you clench your fists and work yourself up and look out over the heads of the people staring up blank vacant mouths yawning open you sweat blood hanging there on the cross the nails ripping open your hands Father let this chalice pass from me the terrible suffering and torture etched on your face but it is for the sins of the world.

I.H.S.

Robert Cook said it meant I Have Suffered.

The goat bleated again in Doherty's Yard. I came from behind the barrow. I could hear the hens again and the birds starting to sing again in the world. Maybe he was wrong. He could be wrong. He could have made a mistake. What I would do was I wouldn't think about it at all. I would wait till I got back home and then get to the bottom of this mystery. I would keep the thought out of my head. There was Lough Swilly and the wee one-track railway and the whole of Buncrana to explore. What I needed was a soda farl with thick creamery butter on it and maybe some home-made gooseberry jam. I ran into the kitchen.

8

The next day I was down at the SWAN MILLS looking over the bridge at the old Ford tin lizzies being loaded with bags of flour when Annie came down to get me for my dinner.

–Come on, my little man, your dinner is ready.

–You've not to call me my little man, I'm getting too big.

–Well, that's what Aunt Annie calls you.

–That's different, she's my auntie and that's only the way she speaks.

–Well, I'm a lot older than you.

–You're not that older and I don't like being called a little man. I'm not that wee.

–You're not the size of tuppence.

–Away, smelly.

–Here. Who do you think you're calling smelly?

–Pee-the-bed.

–You've not to call me that any more. I'll tell Aunt Annie. You'll get it.

–Tell-tale, tell a tale.

–I'll tell her.

–I'll not call you pee-the-bed if you don't say I'm wee and call me my little man.

–All right. Come on for your dinner.

–Wait till this one is loaded.

Then we walked up Main Street towards the shop. Annie said

–Guess what?

–What?

–Some people called O'Toole have come down from Derry to stay with us. Auntie calls them 'paying guests'. The man has got a pub in Derry and there's a baby called Mick.

–*Micky O'Toole from the cabin beyond.*
–What d'ye say?
–*Boys how I envied McGinty.*
–You're daft. The mother is nice. She's got bobbed hair and lovely scent. They've got a nursemaid as well—her name's Nora—to look after the baby and a big pram and the man's got a motor and he's driven away back up to Derry because even though he's on his holidays he has to keep his eyes on the pub, it's called *The Ferryquay Bar*. They've to live on the second floor.

Coming attractions. Next week we present Micky O'Toole and Patrick O'Connor in the stupendous attraction THE MONSTER OF LOUGH SWILLY.

We all went past the Polis Station on our way to the shore. A polisman in the Irish Free State is called a garda and there was one standing at the gate. He winked at Nora and she blushed. There was me and Annie and Nora who was pushing the pram with Mick, the baby, in it. He was quite a good baby who laughed a lot and blew bubbles and didn't give much trouble. It was a great warm day and we were all going for a swim. The road went under some trees and I looked up and saw the sun shining through the leaves and a mystery away up there at the very top. I kept my head back, looking up as we went along until we were out of the trees and had to turn a corner into a wild country lane. Here, the scent from white roses growing on the hedges along the lane made us stop to see if we could pick some but the thorns defeated us. My finger was bleeding but the scent made up for that and stayed with us, mixing with that from some fuchsia bushes further along and the heat shimmering on the road and all this together with the blue mountains that could be seen rising on the far side of Lough Swilly made a kind of strange feeling inside me, like a sort of longing.

We passed an army camp with the green, white and gold flag of the Irish Free State flying from a pole in the barrack square. Some soldiers came over to the barbed wire fence and spoke in low voices to Nora and she was laughing and blushing again. She made us promise not to tell anyone she was speaking to soldiers when we got back home.

Then on to grass and down a dirt path to the shore till we found a place sheltered from the wind. M'mother had got us new bathing costumes from Derry, and Annie and I went to different sides of the pram and stripped and put on the suits and ran down to the sea. When we got in I found that, wet, mine was too big for me and flopped and slapped against me like a belly flapper so I chased Annie and splashed and tormented her till she was screaming.

Later, we sat on the dunes in the sun after we had dried ourselves with the towel and Nora said she was going for a message and would be back soon. Annie was playing with the baby and she turned and looked at me out of the side of her eyes and said in a low voice

–Mind we used to play houses when we were wee-er?

–No, we didn't.

–Yes, we did.

–I wanted to play cowboys.

Annie giggled.

–We got married.

–As if you could marry your sister.

–We had our wee house.

–I could never see it.

–My doll was the baby. We let on we had a house and the doll was the baby. . . . Sometimes you used to give me a kiss.

–I did not.

–You did. I let you have some of my cherries.

–Oh, yeah?

–Yes. You said all right if I didn't tell anybody.

–Well. . . . Maybe we did.

–And the doll was our baby.

–Maybe we did. But you shouldn't tell anybody. Even now. You shouldn't talk about it. . . . You've got ferntickles all over your face.

–It's the sun. . . . I've still got that doll in my case. Maybe we could play houses again, eh?

–I'm too big now. You've not to tell anybody we played houses.

–All right. I'll keep it a secret. . . . I'll show you the doll in the room tonight. I made a new dress for it. Will you?

–Here's Nora coming back.

–In the room tonight when we go up to bed?

–What will you give me?

–Wait and see.

–Something good?

–Yes.

–I'll see.

Nora came up and she had bought us penny cornets from the ice-cream barrow as auntie had given her the money to do and we sat and licked them till they were finished. Then she said to come on childher we had better be making our way back. We returned again along past the army camp up the wee lane through the sweet scent of the flowers and the sun shining through the leaves up where the mystery was at the top of the trees and there was a funny feeling in me all the time, a funny feeling about the day as if it was going on forever.

9

That night it was hot in the bedroom and I lay on top of the bed in my sleeping suit. The sun was going down on the other side of the house and the light was growing dimmer in the room. I had said my prayers kneeling at the side of the bed and now I lay listening to the buzz of voices downstairs and the faint tinkle of the shop bell from time to time.

A funny day it felt as if it was going on forever. Could a day last forever? Maybe days never ended in heaven you were coming out after a swim and lying on the grass in the sun eating an ice-cream cornet forever. A drowsy feeling in the air a muzzy feeling in your head and a warm feeling in your belly you lay day-dreaming watching the clouds going by. You dreamt forever. Heaven was a dream forever.

Annie came in on barefoot from the lavatory. She was wearing a long nightgown. She whispered to me that she would show me her doll and rummaged in her wee case under the bed and brought it out and asked me if I could see it. I wasn't very interested in it and I couldn't see anything special about it but she whispered to come over to the big bed and I could lie on top of that. I went to keep her from girning at me. The doll had on a new dress which she had made with beads sewn all over it. She said to look she had even made it a pair of knickers. She lifted up the dress to show me and said weren't they nice, she wished she had a pair of knickers like that. I said I bet she didn't wear any and she put her hand over her mouth and said oh, I was terrible, she would show me them next time she had them on. I said why couldn't she show them to me now and she said she hadn't got any on under her nightgown. She asked me if I could do exercises, if I could lift my leg up straight into the air and hold it there. I lifted up my right leg and held it. She knelt beside me and caught hold of it and asked me how far it could go back and she pushed it back slowly. She said that was good. Then she said now me, lifting her right leg up and her nightgown going up over her knee. She said now I had to do the same, I was to kneel beside her and push her leg back. I knelt between her legs and helped to push back the right one. She said now the other, let her right leg down and lifted up the left. As she lifted this one up her nightgown slipped farther up her legs till it was over her thighs. She said go on, to push it farther back. Her nightgown was now up off her thighs with just a bit covering between her legs. I felt my belly becoming warm again. It was getting dimmer in the room and I could only see her face faintly. It was going on forever it was this funny day. You dreamt forever. Her leg was up. I was afraid to look down. Was it a sin? The feeling in my belly became hotter. She told me to go on, it could go back further than that. I pushed her leg slowly back. She drew up her right knee. I looked down. Her nightgown was slowly coming up from between her legs. Her belly lay bare and white. She said no I had not to look between her legs. I looked. The room was becoming hotter, the light fading fast. She asked me to lie down beside her and not wake the doll. Her nightgown was still drawn up over her belly. She unbuttoned my sleeping suit all down the front. She was sitting up looking down where she had opened it. Then she whispered quick there was somebody coming up the stairs. I dashed back into my own bed. M'mother came in and whispered she hoped we were asleep. There was no reply. I lay on my back and looked out the window at the sky with the warm feeling in my belly and began to feel drowsy and smelt the sweet scent of the white roses and the fuchsia remembering looking up at the tops of the trees at the sun shining through the leaves where the mystery was with the warm funny feeling in me about the day it was still going on it was going on forever.

10

After breakfast and going out to the backyard to see the horses and playing with the goat for a while and standing in my ganghut giving orders to Billy the Kid and Jesse James to rob the bank at the top of Main Street and sitting in the shop for a while behind the counter watching the people coming in and out I wandered away out for a walk by myself. I went down past the barracks and along under the trees but when I looked up at the tops I couldn't see or feel any mystery and the white roses had a different smell and the air hung still. I turned left at a cross-road away from the shore and walked along and it became quieter and the hedges grew taller till it felt like going into a tunnel. All I could hear was one bird whistling away very high up a lark maybe then a cow lowed. All the time there was this smell of dung and sometimes it was like Dan Craig's piggery back home. The fields were covered with buttercups and along the hedgerows were pink devil's fingers and sometimes bluebells but mostly pee-the-beds.

It was a good job I didn't have to go to confession yet. Aunt Annie was up in Derry to get some stock and see to the Ferryquay Street shop and m'mother never bothered us to go when on holiday as long as we went to Mass. I kicked a stone along the road. A wee cart came towards me pulled by a donkey with a man sitting flicking at its rump with a switch and smoking a pipe. He wore a bunnet with the peak unclasped and nearly hiding his eyes but they gleamed at me from underneath. As the cart was passing he took the pipe out of his mouth and shouted something which I couldn't make head or tail of. Dung juice was dripping from the back and making a long trail behind. The donkey gave me a puzzled look.

But I was just as puzzled as he was. It was a puzzle all right. A puzzle of split biscuits and teapots and people looking at each other out of the corners of their eyes and whispering together and making you turn away and hide your eyes and the nice feeling when you got a kiss from a girl or sometimes a woman like Aunt Annie but even nicer and warmer when you could see up their clothes and you mustn't look or touch them in some places and pretend that you haven't got a teapot and when you saw their split biscuits or their bum it was like being on the chair-a-planes or the steamboats at the fair like going to heaven and kissing a girl was all right just fun but looking at their split biscuit or touching them was a dirty thing and you would have to tell it in confession.

Why did they call it dirty? And if James McAteer was right did m'mother and father do dirty things together? Why was it all right for them? If it was true why did it have to be that the only way people could be born was for their fathers and mothers to do dirty things together? Did they have to go to confession as well? If it was dirty could God not have thought up a clean way? It would save the priest a lot of time and he could get on with the choir practice and the football team.

The road took me right round to the SWAN MILLS again and I looked over the wall down to the big pond that the burn ran into. If you leaned out it made you scared, all that great drop below, you would be drownded. I dropped out of the airyplane but quickly opened my parachute and floated down over the pond, down among the midges and closer to the wee fish putting up bubbles. The men loading the tin lizzies looked up with open mouths to see the great aviator coming down among them. But I climbed back into the cockpit of Colonel Lindbergh's Spirit of Saint Louis which had circled round to pick me up, it was always under my control. Then I swooped low over the mill and bombed first the tin lizzies till they were heaps of smoking metal, the drivers all lying dead around. Then I bombed the big mill buildings to the ground and the whole of Buncrana was covered in flour. A hooter sounded off. Like the rest of the men I clocked out after a hard morning's work and went home for my dinner.

Annie was quite the thing at the table just talking away to Cassie about wanting to be a nursemaid when she grew up and look after children. Missus O'Toole let her take Mick on her lap and she was beaming all over her face and acting grown up. I wouldn't mind a kiss from Missus O'Toole, she has red lips and her diddies are very big, swelling against her blouse, I wish she would let me take one out. I've got to put these thoughts out of my head.

I thought now and again Annie looked at me out of the corner of her eyes. M'mother was very busy in the shop as she had been left in charge of it and Annie had to finish up her dinner quickly and go out and help her. Later, I went in as well and it was great behind the counter with the sun shining in from the street through the window. M'mother had to put the blind down a bit to keep the sun off the allycreesh rolls and macaroon cakes and soor plooms and ogie-pogie eyes. She let me get the tomatoes and bananas from the boxes and put them on the scales to be weighed for the customers. Cassie went upstairs to clean the rooms and make the beds. With everybody busy and paying no atention to me, I slipped back into the passage and keeked through the kitchen door and saw Missus O'Toole giving the baby a suck with her lovely big white diddies out. She looked up suddenly and caught me but she just laughed to me and went on, putting her hand under her nice big soft white tit and giving it a squeeze. Oh, boy.

–She told me she loved me
But oh, how she lied,
Oh, how she lied,
Oh, how she lied.
She told me she loved me
But oh, how she lied,
Oh, how she lied to me. . . .

A fat comedian wearing a clown's suit with big black buttons on the front and a hat that went up into a point like a dunce's cap sang this song. Annie, Nora with Mick in the pram and me were out for a walk, it being the evening now and the shop quiet. We had been right round the town by the back lanes and, coming down Main Street from the top, heard music in the distance then saw a crowd of people standing in the market square. A notice tied up on a lamp-post said THE PIERROTS and a motor lorry was standing, the back being used as a stage. This comedian stood on it and, while singing, stopped every now and again to crack jokes with the audience. But all the time he had this sad look on his face and the people weren't laughing very much. I felt sorry for him and began to laugh loudly every time he stopped for breath.

–I leant her some money to back on a horse,
She took it from me and she gave it a toss.
She said she'd return it
But oh, how she lied!
Oh, how she lied to me!

He ended on a loud note with his arms outstretched but everybody looked as if they were going to burst out crying instead of laughing. I laughed very loudly and kept on. Annie and Nora looked at me as if I was balmy and Annie began to squaver about and try to look as though she was not with me. Nora's face got very red. But Mick in the pram began to laugh along with me and blow bubbles. The comedian looked hopefully in our direction and a few people began to titter around us and nudge each other and point at the baby. I think it might have spread only I suddenly felt my arm being jerked nearly out of its socket as Nora hurried us away in a confloption.

That night Annie and I did exercises in the bedroom again. This time she pulled her nightgown up to her waist. And she put both legs up in the air instead of one. I had to kneel in front of her, grip her ankles and try to pull her legs apart.

She kept them tight together until she made me say that she was the mother and I was the father and the doll was our wean. When I said och all right she let me push her legs open wide. The room was dark but when my eyes got used to the dimness I could see easily.

11

I've got time to read what has been written lately in my jotter.

Monday. There are no picture houses in Buncrana. I wonder how Ramon Novarro is getting on. Aunt Annie took our photos in the backyard with a new camera she bought in Derry and I tried to look like him in *The Pagan.* I wonder how Ken Maynard is getting on and his horse Tarzan in the serial at the Lyric. And Wallace Beery. I read in *Picture Show* that he is to make a picture with Jackie Cooper who was great in *Skippy.* But Frankie Darro is better. He was in *Squareshoulders* and he was a cadet soldier in this big military school called West Point or something like that. Anyway it was in America. The old fella took me to see it when he had a winner—but he kept slipping out for a pint—and that's why he calls me Squareshoulders now and again. He must think I look like Frankie Darro a bit. I'm glad I've got square shoulders. Will Janet Gaynor wait for me? I wonder how the gang is getting on. I got an empty lemonade bottle from the shop and in it I put a piece of paper with CORRABEESTIE written on it and threw it into Lough Swilly. It might sail straight to Ardrossan Harbour and be picked up by one of the gang. He'll wonder who sent it. As I am not going to confession I went into the wee chapel and made an act of contrition. I hope that will do.

Thursday. This is a special day, the twelfth of August. I am up in Derry for the day with auntie and m'mother. This time I came up on THE LONDONDERRY AND LOUGH SWILLY RAILWAY on a great wee train just like a shunting pug back home. The railway had only one track and I was glad we didn't meet anything coming the other way. I was taken by Mister O'Toole to his pub, the Ferryquay Bar, to see the Orangemen's Parade which goes right past his door. I had a great view from an upstairs window which we leaned out of. I had it to myself most of the time for everybody else had to keep running downstairs to the pub which was very busy. The parade took a long time to pass. You couldn't help feeling excited. There were flute bands, one after the other marching along in good order. It was the same feeling that you got from the Pipe Band back home or the Winton Flute Band although it's supposed to be a sin to listen to that one.

I recognised some of the tunes—*Kick The Pope* and *Dolly's Braes*. Men with orange sashes and cocked hats were carrying great big banners beautifully embroidered in gold and purple showing King Billy on his white horse pointing with his sword across the Boyne. I've noticed that Orangemen have a special kind of march.. They sort of slither along on the front of their feet, weaving from side to side. I had heard m'mother talking about the APPRENTICE BOYS of Derry and there they were coming into view, preceded by a band of girl accordionists playing *Derry's Walls*. After a banner with a picture of Sir Edward Carson on it came THE UNITED LOYAL ULSTER YEOMEN OF THE FOYLE who were singing

–Too-ra-loo, we'll kick the Pope,
Too-ra-loo-la-randy,
Too-la-roo, we'll kick the Pope
And make him into candy!

Then there was a choir of boys in red cassocks and white surplices who sang very sweetly and in good harmony too

–Lie down, lie down, you Fenian Count,
Surrender or you'll die!
For the tune they played was Kick the Pope
Right over Dolly's Braes!

It was the best parade I've ever seen in my life.

The shop was at its busiest that day, crowded all the time. After the parade, Orangemen came in, choking with thirst from playing on their flutes and Aunt Annie took pity on them and started doing plain teas at half-a-crown a time as all the restaurants were full.

Very late that night before we went to bed, tired out m'mother was saying

–Glory be to God did you see them fellas all sitting around quite the thing under the picture of the Sacred Heart with the lamp burning in front of it!—And them still with their orange sashes on! And they never blinked an eyelash nor said aye, no nor yis to nobody—Yes, sat there quite the thing and they were very civil, too, very civil men—I was wondering how they were going to react and them not only with the Sacred Heart but the statue of the Blessed Virgin Mary as well—Mind you and I'm saying it but some of them fellas were not bad, not bad at all—Not bad at all—Sure they had their day and that was their day when all is said and done—No, fair's fair, they never looked crooked at any one or anything in here so they didn't and only a wee smell of drink about a few of them—I'll say this for them, they never said a word out of place, so they didn't, not a word out of place.

Auntie said it wasn't the Battle of the Boyne they were celebrating, it was the Siege of Derry when the people inside the walls had to eat rats. Gads.

Well it was all right for me. I got quite a few coppers out of it and a couple of threepenny bits. I haven't counted it all yet. But it was a great parade all right. It was as good as the pictures.

Friday. Michael Todd is the name of the fella from around the corner who comes in to serve in the shop from time to time. Aunt Annie knows his mother who is one of the women with coffee lace who were slabbering all over me when she took me out. He has got shifty eyes. He takes a packet of cigarettes from the shelf whenever he wants and smokes them. He is always singing *If I Had A Talking Picture of You-oo* but he never gets the tune right. He acts as if he owns the shop. I don't like him. I think he is pochling the till. I think Aunt Annie has to be protected from him. I tried to work up the nerve to tell her but she won't listen, she just laughs. What can I do? I would shoot him but I haven't got a gun yet.

Saturday. Back in Buncrana again. I saw Missus O'Toole's diddies again. Then, going up the stairs, I saw her pulling her stocking up. I am getting so many bad thoughts now that I don't know what to do, I can't keep them out of my head.

Later, she gave me a kiss and I have been going around in a daze ever since.

Sunday. Would you believe it, we are going home soon. I don't want to go. Annie doesn't want to go. Nobody wants to go. Back to the old attic and the rotten smells and the cockroaches. I heard from Annie that m'mother had an offer to stay on in Buncrana to look after the shop and later bring the whole family over to live. She could have the shop and the house and she could take in paying guests as well. She would coin so she would. M'father and John could try and get a job nearhand. But she would have to wait for quite a while to work the trade up before they could come over.

But she wouldn't do it. She said she wouldn't be parted from m'father, it wasn't right. Bridget, who has to stay on anyway, pleaded with her. Annie and I girned and girned at her. We cried ourselves to sleep because she wouldn't do it. This time we are going home by boat from Derry to Glasgow and then home by train.

12

Back home but Buncrana is still in my head. As I look around at my own local streets or along the shore or up the hill, I don't seem to be seeing them as I saw them before. It is as if the views are coming through gauze. The great holiday happenings keep jumping in my head and getting in the way of the things I am doing every day. I am glad I can bring it back any time by getting in a corner and clenching my fists and squeezing and going out of myself. In a way it is true about that day going on forever. Buncrana will go on forever.

I am trying to find better words for writing in my jotter. When I write my compositions at school and I hit on a sentence and look at it and know and feel that it is right my head kind of sings. I must try and look at the dictionary more and get better words so that this singing will—well, reach a higher key?

I was searching for a word to describe our stay in Ireland. It took me a long time and I couldn't find one at first. Then I found this word—IDYLL. And it said 'Description in verse or prose of picturesque scene or incident, especially in rustic life; episode suitable for such treatment'. So that's what it was. That would be the word. It was an idyll.

James McAteer asked me how I liked my holidays in Ireland.

–It was great. In fact it was an idyll.

–A what?

–An idyll.

–What d'you mean? What kind?

–It wasn't any kind. It was just an idyll.

–'Thou shalt not have false idols before me.' You know what we were told in the catechism.

–Well, anyway. . .

By this time we had reached the ganghouse. James said he wasn't going in, he would see me again. I went through George Hall's close and up an old stone stairway which wasn't used by anyone since it led to a back door of the Good Templars Hall that had not been opened since I don't know when and was all covered in green moss and had a lock which was rusted.

Just past where this stair turned round, the edges of a roof jutted down so that you could climb on to it and up till you came to a skylight with no window in it. And through this was the ganghouse—The Laft. Robert Cook was guarding the entrance with an old brush shaft ready to bang it in the face of any enemy who tried to get in. He asked me for the password even though he knows me.

–Corrabeestie.

–Corrabeestie.

You went through a hole in the floor-boards near the skylight and this brought you on to a shelf which you crawled along to the end then dropped on to a big bench then on to the floor.

The gang all sat round having a meeting. There was a new member since I had last been there, a boy from Glasgow called Spider Austin. He had been in big gangs in the Gorbals before coming to live here. They all asked me about my holiday and I brought out the bag of sweeties I had been hoarding and shared them out. They made me a captain for that and I had a McEwan's beer bottle top stuck in my jersey to show it. Everybody thought I was great because HUNGER! was one of our war cries. Up on the wall of our ganghouse was a big placard with the word HUNGER in capital letters. That was one of the things you had to swear to fight when you joined the gang. As we could never get enough to eat at home we were always hungry so most of the gang's time was spent proguing for food when we weren't fighting other gangs. It was good in the summer when we raided the orchards and gardens of the big bugs and got apples and pears and sometimes even blackcurrants and redcurrants. There was turnips and carrots pinched from the farms, peeled with a knife and eaten on the spot. In the winter we robbed the chocolate machines in the railway stations by putting in flattened beer bottle tops instead of pennies or breaking open a wooden barrel of pulped fruit in the goods yard and scooping it out with your hands and eating it. Sometimes we would lift a big new potato from outside a fruit shop and when we all had one, go down the Bath Rocks and make a fire and roast them. Some of the gang used to go on a break-in and take stuff home especially if their old fella was boozing his dole money, beating up the mother and leaving the weans starving. But, of course, I could never take anything home, m'mother would have murdered me if she'd known that I had pinched a flea from anybody or anywhere. And that goes for James McAteer as well. Anyway, we two haven't been on any break-ins.

Spider Austin was a right Glasgow keelie and very gallus and he had brought some new ideas with him from the city. He wanted to organise a party to pick pockets at the children's Saturday matinee at the pictures. In the Lyric there was a space between the wall and all the seat rows which you could squeeze through. His idea was to go from the back to the front squeezing through when the lights were out, picking pockets on the way. But the gang turned that down with raspberries. We were not going to go in for picking pockets, that was very sneaky. We wouldn't mind a bank robbery but not picking pockets. It was the big bugs we wanted to rob, not our own kind.

But we took up another idea of his. Taking it in turns you waited outside a shop such as a baker's or a fruiter's or confectioner's or even a chemist's until there were no customers inside. Then you walked in as quietly as possible, not making a sound and stood at the counter. If nobody came through from the back you helped yourself to whatever you could get hold of, sometimes slipping your hand into a glass case or behind the counter. If nobody came you left the shop as quietly as you had entered. But if a customer came in or an assistant came in from the back, you asked if they had any empty boxes for firewood and their answer made no difference because you already had what you wanted in your pocket. If you were spotted lifting something or with your hand in a case, you could always run for it with a good start as the shopkeeper was behind the counter. Anyway, with the gang scattering outside, they never knew which one to chase. All spoils from the raid had to be shared out equally. It turned out we got a few lots of eats this way and we were never caught. Anyway, it was mostly wee boxes of cough sweeties or syrup of figs from the chemists' for they were the quietest and so we had a lot of sore stomachs in the gang and very often the skitters—known in the dictionary as DIARRHOEA.

13

The day of the class monthly confession I plunked the school with Robert Brodie who sits beside me. We had planned it a week before. I wanted to miss the confession this time but I didn't tell Robert that was why I was plunking. The main plan was to get a wee wooden boat each and race them from as far up the Galloway Burn as we could get, right down to the shore. The winner was to be the one that got to the sea first. When it would meet the tide coming in and be driven back then we would take that as proof that it had met the sea.

I didn't want to go to confession because of all the sinning that had been going on in Buncrana. It was worrying me. I was supposed to have committed sins but I couldn't feel that I had done anything bad.

I met Robert Brodie in the Plantation Woods near South Beach Station. We both had our school bags with us containing bread rolls and cheese for the dinner break so we could have these half-way through the race and whatever we could progue during the day. We made our way along the burn to where it goes under a road. Here we stopped to climb a big tree which Robert challenged me to get to the top of. I got up much further than he did, right on to a swaying branch near the very top where, if you looked down, it made your blood run cold. The burn looked very narrow down below. I looked down on the road that crosses the burn and over at the big houses on the other side. I saw a figure at one of the windows. It was a little girl with bright red hair who was looking at me and holding her hand up to her mouth in fear. I waved to her. After a while she waved back to me and we began to laugh to each other. Then I climbed down but as we crossed the road to get to the other side of the bridge and continue up the burn she was still looking out the window and waved to me again till we were out of sight.

We made our way up past the piggery and the unemployed's vegetable plots till we came to another bridge across Eglinton Road. The country began at the other side of this and the burn went through a farm where we were chased by a dog but got away by crossing to the other side. Then through the Mill Glen and across the Dalry Road behind Montfode Dairy. We called a halt there and sat down behind some gorse bushes at the side. But first we had a pee each, squeezing our teapots and making it squirt out in thin jets up in the air as far as we could like firemen fighting a blaze. We couldn't keep from scooshing it on each other a bit but we didn't get much on us. We watched the frothy bubbles floating away to the sea.

Why were some parts of your body called dirty? Why was it called dirty things to look at your sister's split biscuit or your mammy's bum or Missus O'Toole's white tits? If it was a dirty thing to look at Missus O'Toole's tits why was it not dirty to take your mother's tit in your mouth and suck it when she fed you as a wean? Why would it be a sin now to look at the same tit that you had held and sucked? Why did you have to keep some parts of your body covered? Why was a lassie's leg holy up to the knee but a sin from the knee up? Why did you have to steal kisses like crab apples and not get them free since you both enjoyed them? Why didn't boys and girls kiss each other more instead of girning at each other?

We squatted down on the grass. Robert knew how to make a trumpet noise by stretching a blade of grass over his fingers and blowing on it but I couldn't do it. I asked him if he had been to the pictures and he said he had been to see Jack Buchanan in *Goodnight Vienna*, it was all right. He said his uncle was a pilot and when he left school he was going to get him on a ship. Where we were squatting was high up and we could see the town and the harbour with the cranes' jibs and the slips in the shipyard on which a boat lay rusting. Arran was very clear, all bluey and greeny, Goatfell tipped with snow as it always was, Summer or Winter, and some of the houses could be seen in Brodick. There was a tramp steamer lying out beyond the breakwater waiting for the pilot to take her in. I asked Robert if he would be going on a tramp steamer or an oil tanker and he said no, it would be a big one, a liner of the Anchor, Donaldson Line.

Had it been a sin to look at Robert's teapot while he was peeing and for him to look at mine? Why? If God made our teapots along with the rest of us why are they called bad things when the teacher had said that all God's creation was good?

The burn was narrow here and we made it the starting point. Before we started, Robert brought out two big fag-ends which he had found along the High Road on his way that morning and we smoked these. After that we thought of setting fire to the gorse bushes with the matches but they were green and anyway we thought a farmer might see the smoke and chase us and we would have to abandon the race. So we put the boats in the water and held them level till the count of three then they were off. One of the rules was that if your boat got stuck you could only get it free by throwing stones, you couldn't touch it with your hands after the race had started.

Robert's boat got in front round about Montfode and it stayed like that all the way to the Mill Glen. There we decided to lay them up on the bank at the spot reached and have our dinner. After we ate our rolls and a banana I had which I halved with him, we found some orange peel which had been thrown away and ate it. That was the latest thing with us, finding and eating orange peel. Then we progued a turnip from a farm and Robert peeled it with his scout knife. We sat under the trees in the Glen, eating.

–Do you know where you come from?

–Aye. Springvale Street, Saltcoats.

–But, I mean . . . Where . . . How did you get here?

–I walked along the High Road.

–No, but I mean . . . I mean before . . . Where did you come from when you were born?

–I didn't come from anywhere. I've always lived in the same place.

–No, I don't mean that . . . *How* did you get born? I don't believe all the stories you're told. Storks and that.

–Eh?

–You know?

–I've heard a lot of stories as well and I didn't believe them . . . But I found out long ago.

–Did you?

–Aye.

–Well, where did *you* come from when you were born?

–We all came from the same place.

–Where?

–I was found under a bush. I came from under a bush. And so did you.

–Aw, daftie. That's just another story.

–It's you that's daft. I'm not daft.

–You're daft if you believe that.

–God's honour. Fusey knuckle and spit.

–Under a bush? Where was the bush, out in the country?

He started to stick his knife in the grass and pull it out. He spotted some soorocks growing in the grass and began to dig them out so that we could eat them. His face was getting a bit red.

–Do you not know?

–No. Know what?

He dug harder at the soorock.

–The bush is between your mammy's legs.

–Eh?

–You come from under the bush between your mother's legs. It's a bush of fuzz. It's after your mother and father do dirty things together.

I lay back on the grass and turned my head away from him. A bush between your mother's legs. Your father took his teapot which was a dirty thing and peed into your mother's split biscuit which was a bush and another dirty thing and so they were doing bad things together—but why did I get a good feeling when I saw Missus O'Toole's tits or her leg above the knee or best of all, looking down between my sister's legs?—and then after the pee mixed you were made and you were born between your mother's legs from under a fuzzy bush.

We put the boats back in the burn and started the race again. I couldn't concentrate. I kept losing ground. No wonder he was winning.

By the time we got to the Plantation again he was well ahead. I looked at the window of the big house but the wee red-haired girl wasn't there. We found a lot more orange peel and ate it. Then his boat got stuck at a big rock among some branches right in the middle of the burn. I began to creep nearer and nearer. He was throwing stones galore but couldn't shift it and I was heading my boat off the big rocks by throwing stones in front. He got his boat away just before I reached him. But I was going great now and placing the stones well and I passed him under the railway bridge before coming out to the shore. So I won anyway, fuzzy bush or not.

14

So it had come at last. Two by two we walked down the road towards the church. It felt as if my soul, black and barnacled like the puffers in the old dock, had broken its moorings and now breenjed about in my stomach. Overdue for scaling. My throat was dry. Each step brings me nearer. The murderer walks to the scaffold looking at the world around him for the last time.

The priest, on his regular visit around the school, had been chasing up the backsliders and I had been warned by the teacher that I must go to the next class confession.

We crossed the road, marched through the gate up the path and into the church, filling the seats one side then the other in turn until the back ten rows, right and left, were filled. Two confessional boxes, one on each side at the back, Father Mooney in one and Father Reilly in the other. Father Mooney was the priest with the kind of face you would see on the pictures of the martyred saints of olden days, pale faced, suffering eyes, moving about silently with his hands clasped before him, patting your head like the laying on of hands. Everybody wanted to get him. Father Reilly was fat, jumpy with darting eyes behind thick-lensed glasses. I was on Father Reilly's side.

The church was cool and dim coming in out of the glare. A hush had descended on the class, it being a sin to talk or laugh in the presence of God and Miss McPoldy stood by to keep check. You knelt down and examined your conscience and made a list in your mind of all the sins you had committed since your last confession. One by one my class-mates began to go in, mumble mumble, come out, go down to the front, kneel down, say their penance and leave, those waiting moving up one all the time. I was about half-way down my side.

I will make a list in my mind of my sins. When I tell them to the priest he will grant me absolution, not him but God acting through him, then my soul will be no longer scaly and barnacled but cleansed white shining and bright—Oh, it will be so white, oh, my dear children, it will have such a radiance that you would only see in heaven itself, making the saints smile for sheer joy. Oh, my beloved children if you were to leave the church and be knocked down by a motor, you would go straight to heaven like an express train—But supposing you committed a mortal sin by having terrible unholy thoughts between the door of the church and the edge of the pavement, would the express be derailed or would the man in the cloudy signal box pull a lever and switch the express on to another line heading straight for hell?—This is God's glorious gift to your priest that, through His grace, he can grant holy absolution, cleansing the blackened soul—mine?—to a state of holy purity—The sanctuary lamp winking and above that the one white eye of the Blessed Sacrament looking out over our heads but deep into my soul seeing the evil, the dirty things I have done. Outside the door of the church the devil stands waiting, unseen by the passers-by, straight and erect under a big tree, his head among the top branches, waiting to trap the innocents—My little friends, when you climb a forbidden tree, you climb into the arms of Satan—I climbed a big tree with Robert Brodie. Was the devil up there and the little red-haired girl one of his imps trying to tempt me? God was in the Blessed Sacrament and on each side statues of Saint Joseph and the Blessed Virgin Mary. On her face tears. Stare at them trying to make them move. She weeps to see the state of my soul. Has she got a—?—My children, these are thoughts that you must fight against—The devil outside is smiling high in the trees, he feeds me thoughts, the fallen angel always striving to thwart God's holy will—But God in his goodness understands these things my dear children. He understands that they are put there by the devil himself so that he can drag you down to the eternal fire and that is why you must plead for God's forgiveness—Her beautiful face, her red lips, her white slim hands, she holds the Infant in her arms. Did she feed him at her tit? Is that a sin for thinking that thought, is that a bad thought? But thoughts of tits are dirty things, how could the Virgin Mary be connected with dirty things. Has she got—? Is that dirty? She, goodness itself. Thinking good thoughts all the time. No, just plain like the tailors' dummies in the window. Under the blue robes air, light, nothing, goodness itself. Kiss her red lips. I sat on her lap, the tears dripped down upon me. Look, a miracle. The statue cried. Holy water dropped from her eyes. Yes, I saw it. It was Patrick O'Connor sitting on her lap. He must be a saint. Didn't you know he is really Saint Patrick in disguise?—They say the holy saints come down every so often and walk about the streets and you wouldn't know them and they dressed up like a collier or a shipyard worker or any working man. —D'ye mind that fella in Dublin, not that fella, God forgive me you shouldn't call him a fella but a saint, he is now a saint in heaven, Matt Talbot, Blessed Matt Talbot and he used to live in an oul' lodging house, so he did, ah sure and nobody knew it but he was wearing chains under his clothes all the time, I think he's been canonised, I think he worked at the docks—I have to try and keep my mind on examining my soul and keep praying and not let my thoughts wander. That is one of Satan's wiles so that he can lead you into temptation. Does she keep her stockings up with fancy garters? Has she got a—?

God struck me through Miss McPoldy with a punch on the shoulder, gulping, my heart fluttering, how did she know, lifting me under the arm, I, at the end of the row, turning me towards the confessional, his eyes look up at me from behind the spectacles, the purple stole around his neck, his face red and shining, I kneel down between his outstretched knees looking closely at the folds of his black trousers, smelling the nicotine on his yellow-stained fingers.

Why can't he be on one side of the box, hidden behind

the screen, his head turned away and me on the other with the door closed so that nobody can hear? Like the grown-ups do? Why do I have to be exposed, kneeling half out in the open, wondering if everybody can hear what I am saying, thinking of all the space around me, nothing to lean on, nowhere to hide, the piercing eyes above me boring into my soul? It isn't fair. God wouldn't do it like that.

–Pray, father, give me your blessing for I have sinned. It is three months since my last confession.

–Speak up child, I can't hear you.

–Three months since my last confession.

–Three months. Well you must resolve to go at least once a month to confession. A boy of your age should be going once a week.

Are my class-mates listening?

–I was talking and laughing in the church.

–How many times?

–Every time I go.

–You must count up the times.

–Ten times.

–Umrch.

–I told lies.

–How many times?

–Four times.

–Umrch.

–I was stealing apples . . . six times.

–Umrch.

–I was disobedient eleven times.

If one mortal sin damns your soul for all eternity, what difference does it make how many times you commit it?

–Umrch.

–. . . dirty things.

–Speak up, child.

–I—I—

–Come along, child.

–I was doing . . .

–Yes. Go on, my child.

–Dirty things.
–I can't hear you.
–I was doing dirty things.
They must have heard that.
–What kind of things?
–Eh . . . Eh . . .
–Yes?
–Eh . . . I was . . . It . . .
–Was it by yourself?
–Eh . . . No . . .
–Who was it with, then?
–It was . . . Eh . . . It was my sister.
–Umrch . . . Go on then, what did you do?
–Eh . . . We were in the bedroom . . .
–Yes?

A feeling that time has passed, the church emptying. The children at my side of the church start to go to the other priest because that side has emptied while I have been in. The shame of it. Afraid to turn round. Oh God, why did I have to get Father Reilly and not Father Mooney? His eyes bore down on me. The buttons of his soutane are frayed. The nicotine smell is stronger. His thumb is dark brown.
I Have Suffered.
–We . . . We did exercises.
–I can't hear you. You're mumbling.
–We did exercises.
–Exercises?
–Eh . . . We . . .
–What did you do after that? And after that? And after that?
And after that and after that and after that and after that and after that and after that and

The feeling of lightness as you walk out through the porch, Miss McPoldy's eyes looking at you with an expression you have not seen before—mistaken, surely, did she look as if she liked you better now?—bearing a shining white soul out into the fresh air and sun, oh the blessed relief to throw off that dirty black scaly load coiling around your entrails, even your eyes seeming to see better and everything and everyone around you changed to good again.

Yes, but . . .

15

–Please, miss?
–Yes, Patrick O'Connor.
–Please miss, why did Our Lord die for us on the cross?
–He died for us to redeem the world.
–Yes, but why did He have to *die* to redeem the world if He was God?
–That was the beauty of it, children, that He came down into this world and took on human form in order to submit to the terrible torture and crucifixion, taking all the sins of the world on His shoulders.
–Why did He let Himself be crucified?
–It was the evil in the world, the evil in men's hearts that brought our holy saviour to the cross.
–But if God created everything then He created the evil as well.
–As well as creating Man in the image of God, He granted him free will but Man chooses evil and turns away from God.
–Then why did He create free will?
–This is the test of Man, that he is given a choice so that he can choose Good or Evil by his own free will.
–Then could He not have created human beings who would choose good all the time?
–We cannot know God's holy purpose.
–And how did Our Lord redeem Man by dying on the cross if Man is still committing evil the same as he always did?
–He wanted to show the world by His resurrection that He could rise from the dead and this is the promise of the holy faith.
–Yes, but . . .
–I'm sorry, Patrick O'Connor, I must stop there. I want you

all, children, to read that chapter of the New Testament tonight as homework. And we must all pray that God will help our faith, especially Patrick O'Connor.

Miss McPoldy looked at me and it seemed that her eyes were asking me for help.

16

WILLIAM HAINES in ALIAS JIMMY VALENTINE said the board outside the Lyric, they always get the pictures years after everybody else. If I can get another two beery bottles from the old fella, I might be able to get to it. I walked down Hill Street from the Castle Hill where I had been having a fight with Bernard Cunningham. James O'Rourke stopped the fight and said to me after that Bernard would have murdered me, he was three inches taller and twice as broad. I said he wouldn't have been winning if he hadn't rammed my face into the iron pailings around the Drill Hall but, to tell the truth, maybe he was right. Maybe sometimes I am bigger in my imagination than I am in reality. Anyway, Bernard and I shook hands and he agreed he hadn't beat me. The best of it is we are good pals. I don't know how the fight started, something about me making fun of the Cunningham's old bus THE STAR.

I crossed Princes Street and went round the bank corner into Bute Place. The dog came rushing out of the Commercial Hotel and I had to run for my life. When I got in the old fella was singing

–*Oh, look at de schnyder,*
Schnyder how she vos!
Oh, look at the schnyder, the comedian used to sing, who's this it was. Yis, *look at de schnyder*. What's wrong with your face, sonny mick? Your nose has been bleeding by the looks of it. Were you in a fight?

Everybody turned to look at me. Annie gave a funny smile out of the corner of her eyes. John looked up from his paper novel by Zane Grey. M'mother said

–Cripes, Hammut, Mijowl! Come over here, boy till I wipe your face.

–Did you win, boy? Did you beat him, sonny Mick?

–I didn't let him beat me.
John said
–Who were you fighting?
–Bernard Cunningham.
–He's too big for you.
–He butted me with his head. That's why my nose was bleeding.
–What did I tell you, sonny man, about the uppercut? When they put their heads down like that do you bring your fist up from underneath and catch them with the quare uppercut.
–Well, he's got a black eye. I didn't let him beat me. The fight was stopped.
–Ah, you won on a technical knock-out, so you did.
M'mother said
–Here, come and get your tea now. And sit up to the table.
Annie said she was going out to meet Margaret Morgan and left. The old fella sat down beside me and m'mother opposite at the table. She went on,
–I was speaking to Mister Scullion today, the headmaster. He came right over to me and raised his bowler hat, fine gentleman that he is. Yis, a fine man he is, he had a beautiful coat on too, so he did.
–He always dresses well, so he does,
put in m'father.
–He had the great word for you, Patrick, even though, says he, he's a bit wild. And he was telling me that he hoped you'd take the qualifying examination and go on to Saint Michael's College in Irvine and then maybe on to the university itself after that. Says I, sir, there's not much hope of that for we wouldn't have the money to pay for his season ticket up and down in the train and his school clothes and books and all the rest of it.
–It takes us all our time to give you tuppence for your bus every day as it is and a couple of oul' rolls for your dinner with a bit of jam on them, maybe.
–I don't want to go to Saint Michael's anyway. I don't like school.

–Yes, but it's not always what you want yourself. And Mister Scullion was saying to me it would be a great shame if you didn't go on, for you have the brain, so you have. That's what he said.
–You're the quare oul' brainy one, so you are.
–I don't like school. I want to leave it when I'm fourteen and get a job.
–Mister Scullion will be sorry, I'm sure he will and Miss McPoldy as well, I know she wants you to go on, so she does. But sure, you can't do the impossible for, even if you won a bursary, it wouldn't be enough, we just couldn't do it.
–It's a pity you couldn't've become the great scholar and maybe risen to be something in the world and taken us all out of this.
–If I leave school and get a job I can bring in some money. Maybe I could make a lot of money and get rich.
–Aye, there's many's the one has said that before you.

October 14. Plunked school and went down the harbour with Charlie Hands to meet the Arran Boat coming in to see if we could carry any bags. A woman put down her case at the bottom of the gangway and I had it on my shoulder before she could say winky, telling her this was the way to the station, to follow me. I carried it all the way up to the Town Station and she gave me ninepence. I went into the tossing school with this—penny I head them, penny you don't—and won another one and threepence making two bob. But a fight broke out between me and Harry Breslin. His brother and another boy held him back and stopped it or else I would've murdered him. I gave m'mother a shilling and kept a shilling to myself.

October 15. I got to see ALIAS JIMMY VALENTINE. That's a great bit when William Haines opens the safe by listening to the tumblers clicking to save the man who is locked inside while the detective watches, knowing he is giving himself away. It was sad when they led him away at the end. I think when I leave school, I might become a crook like William Haines or the Black Sapper but they would never catch me. I would stop when I had a certain amount and buy a big house and take us all away out of the attic. John could have a garage and Annie could be a mannequin and I would buy Bridget her own shop and everybody could be what they liked.

October 23. They made a lot of us in the gang join the choir to keep us out of mischief, they said. Frank McEvoy, Arthur Murphy, Harry Breslin, Joseph Townsley, Tommy Wilson. But we have some fun anyway, especially when we go behind the organ to pump it. I had Arthur Murphy laughing so much he couldn't keep up pumping and the organ played a bum note right in the middle of Benediction when the priest bowed down before the monstrance. Father Reilly came up afterwards and got me by the ear.

October 26. At choir practice tonight, Father Mooney was taking us through a new hymn he had written himself, *Oft when the Dewy Shades of Even.* He made us go through it about ten times and the last time I thought it was very sad with the sun coming through the window and the birds chirping away outside like in a monastery garden.

Oft when the dewy shades of even
Gather o'er the balmy air.

It nearly made you cry. But Father Mooney was still not satisfied at the end.

As we were going home along South Beach Crescent we went into the front gardens of the big bugs' houses and tore up all the flowers and plants. We tried to uproot a bush and nearly got it out of the earth but a dog came rushing out and we had to run for it.

November 1. As it was Sunday, the gang broke into the shipyard and pinched some carbide for Guy Fawkes Day. When you pour water on it fizzes and you can make it burst into flames. We painted MISTER COLEMAN IS AN AUL BASTARD all over the shipyard offices. We had to keep a good lookout for the polis because Eesky Dan was sent to the reformatory for breaking into the Caledonian Railway Station and they were after us.

November 3. Nearly Guy Fawkes Day. This is the last time I will be writing in my jotter as I am going to try and get a job going round with the papers and I won't have time. I will try and get away from school as soon as I can and make a fortune so we can all get out of the attic. I will start now by plunking school as often as I can and spending the day making tips by carrying bags at the harbour and the station. I can also earn a penny every clear board watching for the polis at the gambling schools. If they are playing pontoons I can maybe now and again get on a side bet on face cards. That's as well as proguing with the gang. At the end of the day I'll give m'mother half of what I got.

FUTURE AMBITIONS

Get your long trousers as soon as you can. Then you can get into the billiard den and learn to play snooker for money like Joe Cunningham who beats them all and plays First Cue for the team. You can get into the big Brag schools. So long, kid.

THE END